A Candlelight Ecstasy Romance™

"YOU'RE COMING BACK," HE SAID, OVERWHELMING HER WITH HIS CLOSENESS. . . .

She put out her hands, not knowing whether she was going to push him away or caress him, but the decision was taken from her. She was in his arms, trapped against the hard contours of his body.

He whispered her name, then tilted her face to his, covering her mouth with a force that left her gasping for breath. Then, pulling her gently to the ground, he covered her face with fierce little kisses as his hands built a fire within her that blinded her to time, place, and reason. . . .

STOLEN PROMISES

Barbara Andrews

A CANDLELIGHT ECSTASY ROMANCE™

Published by
Dell Publishing Co., Inc.
1 Dag Hammarskjold Plaza
New York, New York 10017

Dell ® TM 681510, Dell Publishing Co., Inc.
Candlelight Ecstasy Romance™ is a trademark of
Dell Publishing Co., Inc., New York, New York.

ISBN: 0–440–17522–4

Printed in the United States of America
First printing—January 1983

To Our Readers:

We have been delighted with your enthusiastic response to Candlelight Ecstasy Romances™, and we thank you for the interest you have shown in this exciting series.

In the upcoming months we will continue to present the distinctive sensuous love stories you have come to expect only from Ecstasy. We look forward to bringing you many more books from your favorite authors and also the very finest work from new authors of contemporary romantic fiction.

As always, we are striving to present the unique, absorbing love stories that you enjoy most—books that are more than ordinary romance.

Your suggestions and comments are always welcome. Please write to us at the address below.

Sincerely,

The Editors
Candlelight Romances
1 Dag Hammarskjold Plaza
New York, New York 10017

CHAPTER ONE

Her wedding bouquet wasn't at all what Gina had expected Bruce to give her. She shifted it from one hand to the other, waiting beside the tall, striking man who would be her husband as soon as the couple ahead of them finished their turn. The arrangement of baby's breath and carnations in white and shades of blue was attractive in its way, but she was surprised that he hadn't remembered her passion for rose buds, velvety textured in buttery yellow or delicate pink, never dyed in garish artificial colors as was the often-abused carnation.

Of course, the bouquet probably was part of the Las Vegas wedding package, along with the no-waiting period, paid witnesses, and a professionally jovial proprietor who called himself Reverend Findlay. She hadn't expected anything very special when she came from her home in suburban Chicago to marry the man she loved. The ceremony wasn't important; they couldn't waste any of the precious days he had left before his Navy cruise to plan a family-style sentimental wedding. Being together was all that mattered, and she was delighted that he'd been able to finish his family business in California a day early, even though she'd had a frantic scramble to catch an earlier flight.

It wasn't like Bruce to be so quiet! She glanced at his profile and felt a little better when she saw him bite his lower lip, the first sign she'd noticed that he might be nervous too. Shifting her bouquet again, she reached out to rest her fingers lightly on his arm, needing to touch him, assuring herself that they'd made the right decision. A week was such a short time to make a lifetime decision, as her parents, her brother, and even Claire, her best friend and roommate, had pointed out, and now that she was only minutes away from ending twenty-four years of single life, she was scared.

"I thought you'd wear your uniform," she said, moving her hand restlessly on the sleeve of his linen-textured dark brown suit.

He captured her hand under his strong, firm palm, holding it still.

"So it was my uniform you fell for," he said ruefully.

"That's an awful thing to say," she whispered, aware that another couple had entered the waiting room.

His brows arched quizzically, giving his sharply delineated features a sardonic expression. Even though his tone was teasing, there was no hint of his usual good humor in the slightly downcast dark eyes. When he did smile only his lips changed.

"You wouldn't be the first girl to be dazzled by a naval officer in dress uniform."

Remembering how dashing he'd looked when she first saw him at a party given by one of Claire's friends, she pulled away and gripped the bouquet tightly with both hands. Was that what Bruce's first wife had done, fallen for him because he looked so wonderful in his navy whites? Gina was hurt that he might be comparing her to his first wife just moments before their wedding.

8

"You must think better than that of me," she said, her voice unhappier than she'd intended.

He moved quickly to hug her against him.

"Let's not have our first quarrel before we even say our vows," he said.

Locked against his hard body, she felt her case of nerves subsiding. The last thing she wanted was a quarrel, but it wouldn't be their first.

"Our second quarrel," she reminded him, remembering all too vividly their short-lived but explosive battle when she refused to share his bed before they were married.

"I'm not keeping score," he said. "Do you like your bouquet?"

She was saved from answering by the entry of the reverend's assistant, a plump woman over-dressed in turquoise satin when a Mrs. Santa Claus costume would have suited her better. A newly-wed couple trailed her, walking a little too far apart as though they were teenagers trying to be casual about sneaking into a motel room. Gina decided the commercial marriage-mill atmosphere must affect all the couples who came there. The hurried, secretive mood of the place wasn't at all conducive to romance.

"Jonathan Kenyon and Gina Livingston," the woman read from a clip board. "Reverend Findlay is ready for you, if you'll just follow me, please."

Hearing the name Jonathan read aloud shocked Gina then almost as much as it had when he'd used it to apply for the license. In spite of his explanation that Jonathan B. meant Jonathan Bruce, the first name inherited from his grandfather but never used, it was strange to learn her future husband's full name for the first time on their wedding day. Still, she couldn't love him any less if his name were Rumpelstiltskin.

Reverend Findlay was beaming at them as they approached, trying perhaps too hard to provide a festive mood with his enthusiasm, because nothing else in the small chapel-like room suggested the magnitude of the step they were taking. After working part-time at a flower shop for several years while she studied interior design, Gina was appalled by the dusty plastic flowers stuck haphazardly in pale gray vases sitting on a high table that suggested, but wasn't, an altar. She considered asking that they be removed, but when Bruce caught her free hand in his, she only wanted to get on with the ceremony.

"Now, if the happy couple will stand right here," the reverend said with a great deal of unnecessary gesturing. "Mabel, my missus, will stand up for you, young lady, and Tad, my nephew, is the other witness."

The still-grinning officiant put a great deal of energy into placing the small wedding party in exactly the right positions, and Gina could almost see imaginary footsteps etched on the greenish-blue carpet to mark the spot of each participant. Bruce endured the fussing with uncharacteristic silence. Was he wishing it was over or, chilling thought, regretting that he'd ever suggested marriage?

The reverend made a ceremony of opening the worn little book he used for the wedding, even though he'd long ago memorized the words.

Taking a deep breath, Gina tried to put aside her growing sense of unease, searching Bruce's face for any sign of reluctance or regret. She loved the classical lines of his profile, the strong curve of his chin, his high cheekbones, the intelligence that shone in his eyes, but now, just moments before they were to become man and wife, his lips were tightly compressed, giving him an expression that was foreign to her. Where was the laughing lover who had thrown aside his own plans to spend a wildly exciting week courting her?

He turned toward her then, his eyes studying her features with an unreadable expression.

"You're a beautiful bride," he said formally.

"Thank you."

10

Before, when he'd stroked her long chestnut hair or traced the graceful line of her eyebrows over lively hazel eyes, he'd made her feel beautiful. Now his compliment was so stiff and reserved that it sounded as if he felt obligated to say it.

"If everyone's ready, we'll begin now," the reverend said pompously.

Something's missing, Gina wanted to cry out, but the practical side of her nature, the good sense that had ruled her life almost since infancy, asserted itself. They were both nervous, and this was a depressing way to get married. Once it was over, they'd recapture all the joy and loving and excitement. When she'd first met Bruce, she'd known why no other man had ever tempted her to consider marriage, and a case of premarital jitters didn't change their feelings for each other. He was still Bruce, and they loved each other very much.

The words were traditional and familiar; Gina had been a bridesmaid often enough to remember the ceremony almost word for word. When Reverend Findlay had her repeat the vow after him, her voice was firm and clear. The ceremony was over before all her vague misgivings could crystallize.

"You may kiss the bride," the reverend said with so much satisfaction in his voice he might have been marrying two very old and dear friends of his.

He's a good actor, Gina thought. He probably makes a lot in tips.

It was her first observation as a married woman, and she was sorry it was such a prosaic one. This was a time for beautiful, significant thoughts, but all she wanted to do was get away from the artificial marriage-mill atmosphere as fast as possible. The quick, cool kiss Bruce brushed across her mouth didn't even disappoint her. Of course he wanted to get out of there right away, just as she did. Mrs. Findlay hurriedly ushered them out; business was booming, and two other couples were waiting to go through the cold formalities of a Las Vegas wedding.

"Well," Bruce said when they were outside on the still overheated pavement, "we didn't exactly do it in style, but we're legally husband and wife."

Gina giggled, a release from tension, but she stopped abruptly when her new husband didn't join in her mirth. She needed to laugh at the tasteless little room and the self-important reverend and his wife's too-fussy satin dress, if only to reassure herself that the wedding had really happened. Her sense of reality seemed to be tipped at a crazy angle, and she wasn't sure who she was at that moment.

Bruce stepped to the curb and managed to hail a cab immediately; it had seemed much easier to leave his van at the motel where he'd stayed last night and that morning waiting for her plane to arrive. The early September evening was still hot, and she slipped off the demure little jacket that went with her rather daring backless, white Qiana dress. As she'd planned, removing the jacket changed her bridal dress into a smashing gown for a night on the town.

The effect on Bruce wasn't at all what she'd expected. He raised an eyebrow, but ushered her into the cab without commenting.

"Hungry?" he asked.

"Starved."

It was true. Except for a few bites of toast at dawn, all she'd had that day was tea.

Her husband gave directions to the cab driver and settled back beside her with nearly a foot of space between them. Married couples didn't usually neck in the back seats of taxis, she supposed, but she did feel let down when he didn't touch her. Bruce had never before been reticent about demonstrating his feelings. In fact, the day they'd made a whirlwind tour of Chicago, their kiss in the World

12

War II German submarine had livened up a grade-school tour of the Museum of Science and Industry. Why was he so distant now that they were married?

The crowded streets were surrealistic in the dusk of evening, neon lights playing strange tricks against the darkening hues of the sky. Gina had never been in Las Vegas, and seeing it for the first time as a new, but rather confused, bride, she was both fascinated and repelled by the gambling parlors, pawn shops and garish signs enticing people to gamble, gaze, and gorge.

The hotel where they stopped was almost a relief, its modern lines blessedly unadorned by glowing tubes of glass. Inside, the lobby was moderately crowded, and even her wedding was briefly forgotten as she tried to absorb the scene around her. Visitors in every kind of dress from punk-rock revivals of the mini-skirt to faded cowboy denims elbowed each other indifferently, shopping, arranging for tickets to the hotel's extravaganza, or returning from activities at the pool, tennis courts, and health club. The color red dominated the decor, and the lush casino was the focal point of the action.

"What's your game?" Bruce asked. "Blackjack, roulette, baccarat, keno, craps?"

She laughed self-consciously. "You know I'm not a gambler. I'll leave that to you."

"Because I can afford it?" he asked.

"I'm just a working girl," she joked, not quite sure what to make of his mood.

"You mean you've never had an urge to test Lady Luck? Here." He reached into his pocket and pulled out a money clip, unfolding some bills and offering one to her. "Take a chance on something."

"Fifty dollars! Bruce, I don't want to waste your money."

"There must be something you'd like to try," he urged.

13

"Okay, there is one thing. I've always wanted to work a slot machine, just once to see what it's like."

"There're plenty of those here."

He guided her to a room crowded with machines, many of them being played intently. Except for the continual whir of the machines and calls to the change girls, the room was relatively quiet, the few players welded to the handles of their machines in grim concentration.

"We've beat the heavy traffic," he commented. "You have your choice of several machines. What appeals to you?"

"One with cherries and oranges and things like that, a nickel machine."

"Nickels," he laughed. "It will take all night to lose your stake at a nickel a throw."

He walked over to change his bill, and Gina's eyes followed him. They'd been so close to each other since her arrival that she hadn't really noticed his walk, and what she saw puzzled her. There seemed to be something different about it, not a limp exactly, but a stiffness in his left leg as though he were favoring it. In the few days they'd been apart, he must have done something to it.

"What happened to your leg?" she asked when he returned to her side.

"Nothing much. I just slipped by the pool at the ranch."

"I can't understand why I didn't notice it sooner. You should have said something. Does it hurt?"

"Gina, don't worry. I'm perfectly all right."

He pushed a roll of tokens into her hand.

"These aren't coins."

"When silver got too expensive, some machines were converted to tokens. Don't worry, they'll work in any dollar machine in this room."

"Bruce! I don't want to play for dollars."

"Why not? It's our honeymoon."

"I could lose."

14

"You're not afraid to take a chance. You gambled on marrying me, didn't you? A man just left that machine over there. Maybe he's warmed it up for you."

Reluctantly she dropped one of the tokens into a large slot and watched the reels spin in their glass prison, as from left to right emerged a cherry, an orange, and a lemon.

"A lemon on my first turn. That's not very good, is it?" she asked, studying the combinations needed to win.

"You can't quit after one try," he said when she started to move away from the machine.

"But Bruce . . ."

"Try again," he insisted.

There was a fascination about waiting for the spinning reels to stop that was almost hypnotic, but Gina felt more guilt than optimism as she fed dollar tokens into the machine. Even though Bruce seemed very free with his money, she really didn't know if he could afford to throw it away. Certainly in her family dollars were sometimes scarce, and being out on her own for several years as an assistant to a decorator had made her doubly cautious of her funds. Since she'd have months to wait while Bruce was on his cruise, she planned to return to her job, fortunately being held open for her, and continue living in the apartment she shared with Claire. Until her husband got shore duty, she fully intended to go on supporting herself.

The pile in her hand dwindled very quickly, but Bruce urged her to keep playing. Only a few remained when, to her surprise and relief, a winning combination showed and tokens spilled out. She hadn't hit the jackpot, but she did recover most of Bruce's money. She was glad to get it back.

"Hold out your hands," she said, then counted her take into her husband's palms. "There, I won back almost all of your money. I quit."

"Don't you want to go on playing with your winnings?"

"No way. I owe you seven dollars. That's enough."

"You forget we have community property in my home state. Half of everything I have is yours."

The restaurant's restful atmosphere was very welcome after the hubbub in the lobby and gambling room. When her eyes became accustomed to the dimness, Gina could see the rich mahogany paneling set off by mirrors and crystal chandeliers. Their table was booth-like with tufted leather seats, but latticework dividers made it seem more like a tiny room isolated from other diners. A waiter in a red jacket appeared almost instantly to take their drink orders and present them with a handsome bound menu.

As sips of her frozen daiquiri slid down her parched throat, Gina smiled tentatively at her new, adored husband, watching him toy with his favorite drink, a vodka gimlet. Usually he drank two or three cocktails to her one, but tonight he seemed preoccupied, turning his glass around and around almost distastefully.

"Is there something wrong with your drink?"

"No, it's fine." For emphasis he took a long swallow and smiled. "Are you hungry enough for an appetizer? The scampi looks good, or maybe puffed shrimp."

"Bruce! My shellfish allergy! Do you want me to spend our wedding night in the emergency room?"

"Of course not," he said quickly. "I was thinking of ordering it for myself."

First roses and now shrimp, Gina thought unhappily. How could Bruce forget so much about her so quickly? They'd been apart only a few days while he flew to his family's ranch in California to settle some business with his brother. Before their separation they'd seemed to know each other so well. Was he preoccupied because he thought he'd made a mistake in marrying her? Or had she been the one who was foolishly hasty, agreeing to an immediate marriage when his cruise would separate them after only seventeen days together?

16

"I don't think I want an appetizer," she said, trying to conceal her uneasiness. "After a week of Las Vegas dining I won't be able to fit into my clothes."

"I did want to talk to you about that," he said, looking up from the menu. "I've made other plans."

"What other plans?"

"Would you be too disappointed if we don't stay here in Las Vegas?"

"Bruce, I don't care where we stay as long as we're together, but you were so enthusiastic about honeymooning here."

"Well, I've made arrangements to go to a place where we can be alone for a while."

The idea sounded appealing to Gina, but she was still more puzzled than elated.

"You said you want to pack as much excitement as possible into every day before you go to sea."

"Being with you will be enough excitement."

It was the nicest thing he'd said since their marriage, and she responded with a warm smile.

"Where are we going?"

"It's a surprise."

"Bruce, don't tease. I can't stand not knowing a secret."

"You'll know when we get there."

"Bruce!"

"I'm not going to tell you."

She slipped her foot out of her pump and let her stockinged toes slide up his calf. His face showed disapproval, and she moved away. Sure that no one had seen her gesture in their private little cubbyhole, she was stung by his rejection but even more surprised by it. He had urged her to put aside her inhibitions, and now he was frowning at her innocent attempt to flirt with her own husband.

The waiter returned before she could say anything, and she agreed when Bruce offered to order for her, not really caring what she ate.

His choice, prime ribs, was delicious, but she ate mechanically, her appetite dulled by Bruce's strange mood. He consumed rather than enjoyed a hearty porterhouse steak, keeping his conversation on an impersonal level that required little from her in the way of response.

She just couldn't find an explanation for his attitude. Certainly he didn't seem angry or nervous. How could he regret their marriage when he had urged, even begged, her to agree to it? His high spirits and love of fun, so much in contrast to her own rather serious nature, had attracted her to him from the beginning. Every day that he'd neglected his important trip home in order to be with her had been a zany new adventure, and his sense of humor had made her see familiar things in a new way. Even Claire, who'd thought he was too superficial at first, had eventually been won over or at least silenced by his zestful enjoyment of life.

When she could stand it no more, she tried to probe for reasons.

"Are you worried about something, Bruce?"

"Of course not, darling. Our honeymoon is going to be a memorable one."

In spite of his reassuring words and smile, she still felt something was wrong.

"Bruce, if you have a problem, you know you can tell me."

"I'll remember that," he said solemnly.

Their dinner finished, he ushered her out to the street and into another cab.

Gina had used his motel room to change for the wedding ceremony, but, at the time, she'd been too excited to care whether it was a pleasant room or not. Now, returning to it with her husband, every detail stood out in sharp relief, from the deep rust of the carpet to the reproduction of a Renoir over the dresser. The two oversized beds were covered with quilted spreads in a brilliant gold and dark

18

brown geometric pattern with a touch of the same rust to coordinate them with the floor covering. Her designer's eye mildly approved as she forced her mind to evaluate the room. Concentrating on externals helped mask her disappointment. Surely, when they'd returned to the room, Bruce should have taken her in his arms and said all the things lovers say. Instead he'd left her alone, telling her he'd be back in a few minutes.

She used the bathroom to freshen up, tempted to change into the lovely ivory peignoir set that had been Claire's wedding present. Instead she decided to wait for some sign from Bruce. Maybe there was something on his mind that he wasn't telling her. There had to be some explanation for his remoteness and, yes, even his coolness.

A sharp rap sent her flying to the door.

"Ready to go?" he asked, walking into the room and picking up his suitcase.

"Go? Aren't we staying here tonight?"

"I told you, I've made other plans."

"But I thought . . ." She stopped, not at all sure she wanted to confide in him. How could a bride who'd barely been kissed since the ceremony confess that she wanted her husband to make love to her right away? He could at least act as if he wanted to!

"I've checked out. If you can take your small case, we'll be able to carry everything in one trip."

Instead of opening the rear of his dark green van, he put their luggage behind the front seat. Looking at the sturdy, practical vehicle, Gina realized that it had been her first surprise of the day. She'd expected Bruce to drive a sporty car, maybe a cherry-red EXP or a low slung foreign model with a high-powered engine. Nothing about her new husband seemed to jibe with her impressions of the high-spirited naval lieutenant who'd made her so dizzy with longing that she'd tossed aside all caution for him.

"Bruce, I should tell my parents where we're going."

"Sweetheart," he said, turning to face her, "you're a married woman now. You don't need to check in with your mother and father on your honeymoon."

"I just thought I'd call and tell them we're not staying in Vegas."

"Plenty of time for that later."

He took her arm, boosting her up into the van and firmly shutting the door when she was seated. Following his lead, she snapped the seat belt into place. After one more attempt to find out where they were going, she lapsed into silence, caught up in thoughts and emotions that circled in her mind like a whirlpool. Everything came back to one question: what was wrong with Bruce?

In spite of the roomy comfort of the front seat, she couldn't sit still. The safety belt seemed to imprison her, and she twisted restlessly, unable to settle down. Finally she released the buckle and pulled her shoeless feet up under her, trying to find a position that would be tolerable.

"Remind me never to drive very far with you," her husband joked halfheartedly. "You'll wear out the upholstery, the way you wiggle."

"Sorry," she said, forcing herself to stay in one position. She didn't want him to guess that her squirming was only a symptom of her mind's uneasiness.

Bruce was driving at an even, moderate speed over lightly traveled highway, his headlights cutting through the darkness without revealing much about the surrounding flatland. The night sky was peppered with countless pinpoints of light, and for a while Gina tried to entertain herself by identifying, or imagining that she recognized, different constellations. Her concentration on the stars had one desirable affect: her eyelids dropped until the labor of keeping them open was too great, and she dropped off into a dreamless slumber.

"Sorry to wake you," Bruce was soon saying softly, "but if I don't get some coffee, I'll nod off too."

Awakening slowly, Gina became aware of the firm warmth of his shoulder under her cheek. In her sleep she had cuddled against him, and her hand was still resting on the taut muscle of his thigh.

"I'll talk to you, keep you awake," she murmured sleepily, unconsciously moving her fingers along his leg.

"If you keep that up, this marriage is going to be consummated in a parking lot," he said, when she didn't move away from him.

Awake now but unwilling to be separated from him, she let her other hand wander until her fingers touched the soft hairs at his neck, lovingly caressing them. She heard the sharp intake of his breath just before his lips locked on hers, sampling their sweetness and exploiting their willingness.

Her breath suspended and her senses throbbing, she locked her arms around his body, forgetting time and place. This was a new side of Bruce, more passionate than she had ever dreamed. Now that he had dropped the tight rein on his feelings, he held her against him with an intensity that startled and thrilled her, but also gave her new doubts about herself. With her lack of experience and natural reticence, how could she possibly please the man who was holding her in this new and demanding way?

His hand caressed the smooth skin of her back, then slipped around to gently fondle her breast. His touch brought tingles of sheer joy and quieted her self-doubts, making her realize that his pleasure was dependent on hers. He moved his lips as he kissed her, leading her to respond to the rhythm of his demands with a sureness that made her oblivious to everything but him.

As suddenly as he had begun, Bruce pulled away, leaving her shivering with expectation and desolate at his departure. Watching him walk toward the doorway of the small truck-stop diner, she became more and more upset, impatient with his secretive plans and disappointed by the

21

abrupt way he stopped kissing her. Why couldn't they begin their honeymoon like any normal couple, in a comfortable, private motel room? Why were they racing who-knows-where in the middle of the night to some unknown destination? Why had Bruce kept her at a distance all evening, and why had he left her longing for him with every atom of her being?

Remembering how he had pressured her to respond to his advances before they were married, she couldn't help but feel angry. When would he decide he was ready to act like a real husband?

His kiss proved that he was anything but indifferent to her; when he stopped dangling her at arm's length, he would find he'd have to woo and win her all over again, cruise or no cruise. What little satisfaction she derived from these fantasies was cold comfort for a new bride. She wanted her man beside her, warm, loving, and caring, and she just didn't understand why Bruce was acting so peculiarly.

When he returned carrying two styrofoam cups of coffee, she decided to play the game his way, even if it meant pretending that nothing was wrong between them.

"Do you want your coffee black or with cream?" he asked.

"Neither. I prefer tea."

"Sorry, I forgot. I'll go back for some." His voice was that of a stranger.

"No, I really don't want any."

So fully awake now that her eyes felt glued open, she tried to think of all the possible reasons for Bruce's strange behavior. Of course, she could have been deceived by his lighthearted courtship, but she was sure he hadn't been putting on an act for her benefit. He couldn't have concealed his real self from her; there had to be some reason for his altered behavior. What could have happened in the days he'd spent with his family, or more specifically with the person he'd gone to see, his brother?

"Bruce," she asked hesitantly, "was your brother opposed to our marriage?"

"He didn't say anything against it," he answered in such a calm, matter-of-fact way that she almost had to believe him.

"Did your parents object?"

"No."

The next question in her mind was harder to ask, but she was too troubled to back off.

"Are you sorry you married me?"

"No, Gina, I'm not sorry."

The words were right, but his nonchalant answer didn't satisfy her. He didn't say he needed her, loved her, desired her, cherished her. None of the reassurances she needed came, only a flat statement of fact. She gave up, deciding to wait and see. They were both tired and edgy. The love they felt for each other was real, so things had to work out. The warmth of his kisses and caresses told her that he was anything but indifferent to her.

For a long time neither of them spoke, but gradually Gina's curiosity about their destination surfaced again.

"Can you tell me now where we're going?"

"You'll see when we get there."

"Are we still in Nevada?"

"Your sense of direction is out of whack. We're in Arizona."

Approaching headlights were less frequent as time passed, and eventually the monotony of night driving got to Gina. She dozed, her head resting on the back of the seat this time, not on her new husband's shoulder.

23

CHAPTER TWO

Groggy but aware that something had changed, Gina shook off her sleep. The car window was open on Bruce's side, letting cool air, heavy with the fragrance of pines, blow across her face. Even in the pre-dawn murkiness she could tell that the roadbed was hard-packed dirt, narrow and winding, pitted with potholes.

"Where are we?"

"Nearly there."

"You must be tired," she said.

"That's an understatement."

"It wasn't a very good wedding, was it? The room was kind of depressing."

Las Vegas and the wedding were behind them, but her confusion wasn't. She was pleading for Bruce's reassurances, even though she wouldn't admit it, not even to herself.

"Would you have liked a big wedding, a reception with a champagne fountain and heart-shaped molds of pâté de foie gras?" he asked her.

"How about swans sculpted in ice?" Her laugh was a

24

little forced. "Or maybe a recessional under crossed swords?"

"You are getting carried away."

"No, I never wanted any of that."

She didn't add that she wanted a husband who would love her to distraction, always and forever.

Feeling grubby and stiff, she stretched vigorously then squirmed to straighten the flared skirt of her dress that had bunched up high on her thighs. With her toes she groped for the shoes she'd slipped off at the beginning of their trip.

"Can we stop soon?"

"There's no place to stop between us and our destination, just deserted road and trees."

"Bruce, I really need to stop!"

"Here?"

"Where are we? You didn't tell me we were going into the wilderness. Isn't there a gas station or something?"

"I'm afraid you'll have to rough it. I probably should have told you that our last stop was also the last station, but you were sleeping so soundly I hated to wake you."

He halted the van in the road without bothering to pull to the side.

"You're parked in the middle of the road," she said.

"No one will be coming this way."

She hesitated, not at all comfortable about getting out in the middle of nowhere.

"It's still so dark," she said.

"It's beginning to get light. Didn't you go to Girl Scout camp when you were a kid?"

"No, I spent my summers taking classes at the art center and working my paper route. I'm a city girl." Her laugh fell off weakly.

"If you're afraid, I'll get out with you."

"No," she said, letting the door swing outward.

25

He reached in front of her to open the glove compartment and handed her a flashlight.

"Just don't go far from the road."

Dropping down from the seat in her spike-heeled wedding shoes, she managed to turn her ankle painfully, but she limped toward the woods biting back her groan. Somehow she managed to accomplish her somewhat urgent mission and get back into the van, but not before she shredded the leg of her panty hose on a treacherous low branch.

"Are you sure we're going on a honeymoon?" she said climbing back onto the seat and surveying her demolished hose. "If we're staying around here, I'll need a survival kit, not a trousseau."

"You said it doesn't matter where we stay as long as we're together."

"But we're not anywhere," she cried out in real distress as he guided the van forward, seemingly hitting every spine-jolting chuckhole in the way. "You said you like big cities and crowds and entertainment."

"And you thought our marriage would be one long carnival?"

"Bruce, you're not acting like yourself. I almost feel I don't know you."

"Maybe you don't," he said dryly.

Dawn came quickly. Gina strained to see more of their surroundings, but the woods on either side frustrated her attempts. The van was climbing, of that she was sure, and the road was getting much worse, narrowing to little more than a crude trail. If they met another vehicle head-on, they were in big trouble. It would be a delicate maneuver to let even a small car pass the bulky van.

The van was barely moving, straining to make a steep incline, laboring over a trail that barely accommodated its width. Gina expected to have the metal side torn away by the trunk of a gigantic tree at any moment, but suddenly they were in a large flat cleared area with enough space for the van to swing around in reverse.

"This is as far as we drive," her husband said, turning off the ignition and opening his door.

"There's nothing here."

"Right and wrong. This is as far as the van can go, but a few hundred yards up that trail is our honeymoon cabin. You'll never make it in those shoes, though. I hope you have some that are more practical."

"Yes, in my biggest suitcase," she said, fighting the disappointment she felt looking around the little clearing in the woods. "How long are we going to stay here?"

"That's up to you," he said, taking out her suitcase and sliding it onto the seat so she could open it.

"And if I vote to leave now?" she asked dejectedly.

"Sounds like a case of poor sportsmanship."

"It does, doesn't it," she admitted. "You've just caught me off guard, Bruce. A week at the North Pole wouldn't have surprised me any more than this. I'm sorry. I should at least give it a fair try. If you enjoy being here, maybe I can learn to like it."

"It wouldn't hurt to try," he said, but he sounded strangely indifferent as he continued removing pieces of luggage from the van.

When her sturdy shoes were on, looking ridiculous with her torn hose and stylish dress, Gina leaned over the seat to watch him, really noticing all the bundles and boxes in the rear for the first time. Because she hadn't connected them with their honeymoon, she'd scarcely given them a thought.

"Does all this stuff have to be unloaded?"

"Yes, and carried up the mountain. Take this smaller suitcase on your first trip."

The stiffness in his leg must have been aggravated by the all-night drive, but it didn't slow him down on the steep slope. He raced ahead of her, leaving her to scramble for

27

secure footing on a course that wove its way through tall timber. Spongy underfooting from countless seasons of falling pine needles, the pathway existed mostly in Bruce's mind, and the light of day barely penetrated the huge overhead branches. Winded, her ankle throbbing, and her hand aching from the weight of her suitcase, Gina finally caught up with Bruce when he was already inside a small log structure. Her misgivings grew as she joined him in the dim interior. Appalled by the smallness and crudeness of their honeymoon cabin, she felt an unwelcome tightness in her throat. She struggled for something positive to say but came up empty.

"Why are the windows so high and small? It looks like a fortress to fight off Indians."

Her attempt at humor fell flat.

"To discourage animal marauders, especially bears. I'm also careful not to store any food here when the place is unoccupied."

The total floor space of the single room wasn't much greater than that of her apartment living room. An upper and lower bunk were built against the far wall, each one holding a plastic-covered double mattress, the only small concessions to comfort in the whole room. An unfinished plank table and several mismatched chairs dominated the center of the room, and the bare boards of the floor felt slightly gritty underfoot. A small pine chest of drawers, a modest-sized cast iron stove, and a metal cupboard with shelves completed the furnishings in the bleak little room.

"How did you make all this?" she asked, gesturing at the cabin in general.

"The cabin? I built it and hauled everything up here over a period of time. It's taken me five years to get it the way I want it."

"I'm so . . . surprised. Why did you build it, Bruce?"

"It's time you know, I guess. I'm Jon."

"What?"

28

"Jon, my name is Jon, Jonathan Bradford Kenyon, not Bruce."

"What are you saying?"

She shivered, the dawn chill more noticeable now that the uphill climb was over. Her husband was staring at her intently, and she desperately tried to think of an excuse for his strange words and gaze.

"Several times I thought you were suspicious," he said. "I goofed badly on your shellfish allergy. Bruce would have known about it."

"What are you telling me?"

The words choked her, and she felt all her misgivings rise up to haunt her. Something had been wrong from the beginning, but she couldn't believe what she was hearing.

"I'm not Bruce."

"You have to be," she cried out in anguish. "We're married!"

"Yes, legally bound to each other for as long as we remain on this mountain. Gina, don't you know anything about the man you wanted to marry? Didn't Bruce tell you he has a twin?"

"You're his twin," she said woodenly, too stunned to look away from his face.

Bruce had talked about his brother, usually in a faintly exasperated way, complaining about his only sibling's stern and serious nature. Gina had imagined him as an older brother, a crusty bachelor too wrapped up in his business to care much about his brother's concerns. She couldn't remember Bruce ever mentioning his name, and she had, in fact, dreaded meeting him more than Bruce's parents, who apparently doted on their son, the naval officer.

"You're married to me, not Bruce, but it's only a temporary arrangement. You don't need to look at me like that. I'm not an ax murderer. As soon as Bruce is safely at sea, we'll have this farcical marriage annulled. You

29

won't get the settlement Bruce's first two wives got, but I'll see that you receive generous compensation after you sign an annulment agreement."

"Two wives?"

Gina was visibly trembling now, but whether from cold or shock she didn't consider. In her heart she knew the man in front of her was telling the truth, but the blow was too bitter to absorb.

"Oh, no!" He shook his head. "You don't even know Bruce was married before?"

"He told me about his first wife," she said, defying him now to save herself from getting hysterical. "A foolish first marriage doesn't matter. He was too young then."

"He was twenty-four the first time and twenty-nine the second time, only two years ago. His so-called career in the Navy makes it easy for him to slip in and out of relationships, but it's too damn expensive for the family."

"Why did you trick me into marrying you? Does Bruce know?"

"When he gets to Las Vegas today he'll think his bride-to-be got cold feet and jilted him. I sent your parents a telegram saying you'd changed your mind and needed time alone. Bruce was generous with his information about you. He even showed me a photograph. But after a few days of pouting he'll go on to his next conquest."

"I don't believe you!" she cried out, fighting the pain and anger. "I've got to go back to Las Vegas immediately. I can't stay here alone with you."

He frowned, the expression on his face turning her heart into a block of ice.

"Gina, you're my wife, and this is our honeymoon. Bruce will be safely at sea in seventeen days. Until then this is where you stay."

"You can't keep me here!"

"I can. The only keys to the van are on my person right now, and you won't have an opportunity to get them.

30

Your chances of walking away from here safely are about twenty to one, even if I don't follow you. I will follow. You have to stay until I take you back. You can be sure of that."

Once, when she was still in grade school, their family dog had cornered a wild rabbit, a hardy city-dweller usually wily enough to avoid its four-footed enemies. She'd been proud of saving the trembly little creature, but now she remembered the incident and knew how it felt to be the prey, overwhelmed by an impossible situation and helpless to fight back. No one could rescue her; tears spilled out, draining some of her rage in the only way left open to her.

He left her alone in the dreary cabin, returning with another load of supplies, then leaving and returning again and again. She didn't keep track of his trips, but every time he came into the room she wanted desperately, savagely, to strike back at him. He had robbed her of the man she loved and mangled her self-respect, making her feel like a hopeless idiot for marrying the wrong brother. Not only couldn't she distinguish her fiancé from his brother, she'd been forced into admitting she didn't know Bruce had a twin or a second wife. Humiliation and disappointment fed the fires of her despair.

His trips seemed to go on forever until the room was crowded to capacity with boxes, bundles, and suitcases. He only spoke once when he handed her a nylon jacket and suggested she put it on. Eventually she pulled it across her chest as she huddled in a corner of the lower bunk in a stupor of misery, but no external covering could make her feel warm.

He didn't suggest that she help him put things away, and she didn't offer; instead she watched him with total loathing. How could a man who looked exactly like her beloved, adored Bruce be such a devious, conniving person? She detested him so much that her head pounded in agony and her eyes felt like burning coals.

31

"Why?" she finally asked in a strangled voice.

"It wasn't something I wanted to do."

"You've ruined my life!"

"No, you'll leave here wiser and wealthier."

"What right do you have to interfere in Bruce's life or mine?"

"None, if what you do doesn't affect my family, but Bruce has already sliced up his share of our land. Three costly divorce settlements are three too many."

"I would never divorce Bruce. I love him."

"You think so now, but what I'm doing may be better for you too. Bruce will never settle down to a nine-to-five shore job, and a wife is the last thing he wants if he gets the foreign assignment he's been angling for."

"That's my worry and Bruce's, not yours. You have no right to interfere."

"My brother handed me all the responsibility for our family's business when Dad's health forced him to retire early. If Bruce wants to get the benefits without working for them, he'd damned well better grow up."

"That has nothing to do with our life together. I have a job, and Bruce has his Navy pay."

He put aside the case of canned goods he was stacking in the metal cabinet and stepped around the many obstacles on the floor until he stood towering over her. Even knowing that he wasn't Bruce, she couldn't pick out any distinguishing differences in his physical appearance.

"You look exactly like him," she said miserably.

"Yes, I do." His voice was low and not unkind. "We can fool our parents if we both keep our mouths shut. But believe me, the resemblance is only skin deep. We differ in almost every other way. Do you really believe Bruce lives on his Navy pay?"

Refusing to look at his face, she only nodded her head, dreading to hear that there were other important things she didn't know about the man she wanted to marry.

He swore softly under his breath, and she pushed her back against the rough log wall to put more distance between them. When he sat down on the mattress and stared at her with searching eyes, she felt afraid of him for the first time.

"I can't stay here alone with you."

"You don't need to worry about my intentions," he said patiently. "I want a bona fide annulment based on sexual incompatibility. You couldn't be any safer if I were a monk, not that I think you're as innocent as Bruce tried to make me believe. And don't waste your time trying to convince me Bruce is just a poor misunderstood boy."

"You are so cruel," she said, pulling the jacket more tightly around her.

"Not cruel, realistic. I don't want another ex-wife grabbing off Kenyon assets, most of which are tied up in land, as I'm sure you know."

"The only thing I want from the Kenyons is the man I love."

"You'd turn down a nice peach orchard in the San Joaquin Valley or maybe some vineyards? Or how about a winery?"

His skepticism forced her to defend herself with the only weapon she had, the truth.

"All I know about Bruce's family is that they live on a ranch."

"Come on, Gina, I'm not a total fool. The Kenyon ranch is a large-scale fruit farm, over six thousand acres of prime orchards and vineyards with packing plants, canneries, a winery."

Staring at him as though he were speaking a foreign language, she was too surprised to react.

"Surely Bruce threw a few statistics your way just to perk up your interest. Didn't he mention that close to a million crates go down our conveyors every year or that we employ nearly five hundred workers just packing

33

plums at the peak of the season? He usually exaggerates our holdings when he's trying to impress a woman, so you can't expect me to swallow some story that you thought you were marrying a poor sailor."

"You are so wrong. How can you be related to someone as kind and wonderful as Bruce?"

Even though she was determined not to let him see any more tears, she couldn't choke back the quiet sobs that shook her body. In only a few hours the man she loved was going to meet the plane that should be bringing her to their wedding. When he called her parents, as he surely would, he'd be convinced that she didn't love him. Never, ever, would she forgive Jonathan Kenyon for doing this to Bruce, to both of them.

His voice seemed to come from far away, although he was still sitting on the edge of the bed.

"It won't make you feel any better," he said softly, "but I don't like what I had to do. My father's health is precarious, and he just isn't up to another tense, unpleasant divorce. Mother thinks Bruce is the perfect son, but Dad has had to use his influence too many times to keep him out of trouble. The Navy was Dad's idea, a way of keeping Bruce out of jail."

"I don't believe that!"

"I don't expect you to, but California has pretty strict laws about fifteen-year-old girls, even overly ripe, willing ones."

"I won't listen to any more of this!"

She buried her head in her arms and wept without restraint, more unhappy than she had ever believed possible.

Eventually either exhaustion or a sense of total futility won out, and Gina slept deeply, not awakening until late afternoon. She was lying under an open sleeping bag that had been unzipped to serve as a blanket, her head cradled on her arm. For a long while she lay absolutely still, as though she could will away everything that had happened and find herself back in time twenty-four hours earlier. The cabin was silent, and she seemed to be alone. Slowly she rolled over to face the small room, now less cluttered and definitely unoccupied.

Gradually sitting up, she found that her shoes had been removed and placed neatly beside the bed, but knowing her unwanted husband had made this gesture didn't soften her feelings toward him. He had no right to touch her!

Except for her own luggage, all of the gear from the van had been neatly stowed away, even though it meant hanging clothing and other items on hooks imbedded in the log walls. She didn't know where Jon was, but she was going to take advantage of every second he was gone. First, she wanted to get out of her wedding dress and burn it to ashes so it would never remind her of the mockery of her wedding again. If only she'd had enough confidence in herself to pay attention to her own misgivings, she might have avoided his deception. Looking back, dozens of little things about Jon had seemed strange, but she had been so full of her feelings for Bruce that she let his brother's appearance deceive her, ignoring the warnings his personality gave.

Not knowing where Bruce's sense of adventure might lead them, she'd packed for every type of activity, fortunately including two pairs of jeans. If not today or tomorrow, then the next day, she was going to get out of the trap Jon had sprung on her, even if it meant hiking back to wherever civilization was. He'd been clever, letting her sleep during the drive, so she had no idea where she was; but the road that brought them to the cabin had to lead to other people eventually. He couldn't stay awake to watch her twenty-four hours a day, and when he wasn't looking, she'd be gone. Four flat tires on the van would give her the time she needed.

A big kettle of water was starting to warm on the cast

iron stove, and she dipped some out into a small pan to wash her hands, drying them on the skirt of her soon-to-be-burned dress. A long steamy shower would seem paradise, but she couldn't waste time wishing for an impossibility. Dressed in a complete change of clothes including her canvas sports shoes and a forest green sweater, she felt more in control of herself and her destiny. All she needed now was a good meal and an opportunity to escape.

"You're awake," Jon said needlessly, coming into the cabin with an armload of firewood just as she was poking her dress into the fiery interior of the stove. "Our meals won't be fancy, but we won't starve either. After tonight I'll catch enough fish to keep us going, but tonight you'll have to settle for canned chili. What are you burning?"

"It's not your concern. Is there a bathroom here?"

Her voice was deliberately toneless. He'd seen the last of her misery. From now on every speck of her energy was going to be used in getting away.

"There's an outhouse in back and a fresh mountain stream not far from here that will serve as our water supply and bathtub unless we get some rain. It's been a dry year. There's not a drop in the cistern."

Gina didn't intend to be there long enough to worry about the water supply, so she walked out of the cabin without saying anything else.

The last thing she remembered from their drive was that they were in Arizona, and the deeply timbered retreat was probably in the mountainous part of that state. Her nostrils weren't accustomed to the pleasantly biting scent of pines and the cool freshness of the high country, but she sucked in air gratefully, letting it clear her head and combat the achy feeling left over from her crying.

The stream was picture-postcard perfect, a boulder-strewn creek that fell rapidly downward from a small waterfall a few hundred feet above. The water she splashed on her face still carried the iciness of last season's high snows, and she couldn't imagine bathing in it. Her skin felt shivery as she sprinkled it on her face.

After making several circuits of the cabin, she knew all there was to know about leaving it. The stream and the high ground cut off her escape on two sides, and the third route was blocked by a treacherously deep ravine. The only way to leave was the way she'd come, downhill past the van. She hadn't seriously considered striking off alone into unfamiliar and almost certainly dangerous woods, but the fact that she couldn't manage it if she wanted to was depressing. The only safe way to leave was to follow the wretched roadway below the van, and it would be much too easy for Jon to track her that way. She had no idea how far she'd have to walk before finding a fork in the road or some sign of human habitation. Her plan seemed much more difficult as she studied the truly wild nature of his retreat. Her only hope for success lay in leaving just after he fell asleep that evening, giving the van four flat tires, and walking all night.

Only her raging, unchecked anger gave her enough courage to plan her escape seriously. The awful things Jon had said about Bruce were burned on her brain, and she had to get away from the man who'd made wild accusations about her fiancé. Only by finding Bruce could she sort out his brother's half-truths and lies, and time was one thing she lacked. Even now Bruce would be experiencing his initial disappointment when her scheduled flight arrived without her. Would he wait for the next plane or call her roommate or her parents right away? Claire was taking some vacation time to visit her aunt in Minnesota, so Bruce would call her parents for sure. Would they be suspicious of Jon's telegram? She never sent telegrams; wouldn't they wonder why she hadn't called instead?

Kicking at a stone, she only managed to hurt her toe and remind herself that her twisted ankle was a little sore. Walking in the dark on that rutted road was going to be miserable at best, and she was starting off with a bad ankle.

Her parents wouldn't doubt the telegram. Kind as they were, they'd just assume she was too upset to talk to them. They'd tell Bruce she'd changed her mind, and then where would he go? Would he go back to his family home where she could reach him or try to dull his unhappiness by going somewhere else? Or would he haunt Las Vegas hoping for some word from her? As much as she longed for the latter, she didn't dare hope for it. He would be hurt, maybe offended, certainly disappointed, but did he love her enough to believe that she hadn't run away from him?

After another restless circuit of the clearing around the cabin, she miserably admitted that she couldn't predict what Bruce would do. Their time together had been terribly short and totally filled with their feelings for each other, but there was so much she still had to learn about the man she loved, if she ever had the chance.

Jon's horrible innuendos bothered her, but she refused to believe them. If Bruce had been too ashamed of his marital record to confess to both marriages, it could be a measure of his feelings for her. Lots of young men made mistakes. He just cared too much about her to let the past come between them. She wanted to believe that. Dear God, how she wanted to believe it!

Her headache was growing worse in spite of the invigorating air, so much cooler than the desert air of Las Vegas, yet drier and crisper than the humid atmosphere in her home state. A meal might make her feel better, but that meant facing Jonathan Kenyon. If it weren't for her plan to escape, she would refuse to touch his food. Let him explain to his brother that he'd both tricked and starved his bride-to-be.

The stove-heated cabin felt good; her hands had gotten stiff with cold as the sun sank out of sight. Jon was just taking a pan of muffins from the oven, looking so much like Bruce that her heart missed a beat. If only he were Bruce, she wouldn't mind honeymooning in this remote spot. She needed Bruce so badly at this moment that she nearly broke her resolution not to cry again in her captor's presence.

Wearing faded jeans and a plaid flannel shirt open at the neck, he looked different from the way he had in his carefully tailored suit. Did she only imagine that his shoulders were a little broader than Bruce's and his waist a little slimmer? The arm that carried the pan looked granite hard, accustomed to heavy lifting but, of course, a rich man's son didn't have to do manual labor. Maybe she was only imagining differences between the twins because she wanted this man to be totally unlike the brother she loved.

"Dinner's ready," he said formally. "I'll do the cooking until you learn to handle the stove, but the rule of the wilderness is that everyone pitches in."

She didn't have enough energy to defy him, but only her escape plan kept her from walking out of the cabin, hungry or not.

His face across the table was composed but unreadable. Was he sorry for what he'd done, or did he only regret that he had to stay there with her until Bruce was safely at sea?

The meal was good, she supposed, but her anger gave every bite bitter seasoning. At least he didn't make any small talk; she didn't think she could bear an attempt to make the meal seem like an ordinary one.

She did learn one thing. He kept several keys on a sturdy-looking chain around his neck; one of them could be the van key. What were her chances of getting it after he was asleep? If he used the upper bunk, could she reach up and remove it without waking him? How much easier it would be if she could leave in the van. She might even reach a phone in time to catch Bruce in Las Vegas. She didn't know where he was staying, but maybe the police would help her find him. Wasn't it some kind of crime to trick a person into marrying you?

"You're staring at my keys," he said wryly. "Forget it, Gina. You don't have a chance, and just to save myself from the possibility of being choked in my sleep, I'll tell you these aren't the van keys. You can search the cabin for weeks without finding them. We old Indian fighters know how to hide things."

"You are despicable," she said, her appetite ruined before it was completely satisfied. "It's against the law to kidnap people."

"A man hardly has to kidnap his own wife on their wedding night, or have you forgotten that you're Mrs. Jonathan Kenyon, signed and witnessed?"

"In the sleaziest wedding ceremony ever devised by man."

"If you hate Las Vegas-style weddings, why did you let Bruce talk you into one? The waiting period in most states is only a few days."

"With Bruce it would have been a lovely wedding. It was your attitude that ruined it."

"Why didn't you question it at the time?"

"It doesn't matter now."

"We're going to be together for at least seventeen days. Wouldn't it be better to get your resentment talked out so we can coexist peacefully?"

"What do you mean, at least seventeen days?"

"Seventeen days if you sign the papers I need for an annulment."

"And if I prefer to bring criminal charges?"

"What charges? It doesn't matter. You're staying here until you sign."

"How can we get an annulment after being together for seventeen days?"

40

"Seventeen sexless days will do it. If this presents any particular problems for you, say so now."

Her face flushed as a fresh burst of anger assailed her.

Surprisingly, he quickly apologized. "I'm sorry. I don't want to antagonize you more than I have already. I know you're hurting, and my crude attempt at humor was out of place. But I still think you'll thank me for this someday."

"Never!" She stood and pushed her chair away so violently that it crashed to the floor behind her.

He calmly continued eating, but Gina had to get away from him. She slammed the door of the cabin as hard as she could, but the thick planking and the heavy log walls resisted the impact; all she managed to create was a dull thud.

Watching the water of the stream dash over concealed and protruding boulders, she managed to make her mind a blank, rallying her strength for the escape attempt, as she called it. It was nearly dusk when she returned to the cabin, planning to be as quiet and unobtrusive as possible for the rest of the evening. Jon had to be tired; he'd driven all night and apparently worked around the cabin all day. It wouldn't be hard to outlast him, and once he was asleep, she'd gather her money and some food and be on her way. Unfortunately, she believed him about the van key being hidden, but the one object she needed for the success of her plan was a sharp knife. Slashing the tires was the only way she could think of to put the van out of commission long enough for her to reach help.

"I've cleaned up tonight," he said when she came in, "but tomorrow you should start doing your share. The time will pass more quickly if you keep busy."

She had no intention of being there long enough to do anything in the cabin, so there was no point in arguing. Her immediate problem was to stay awake while he fell asleep, and her long day's nap gave her an edge. He couldn't conceal the fact that he was beat, even though he turned his head so she couldn't see a revealing yawn.

"I brought a bunch of paperback books. There should be some you'd like to read. Other than that, the cabin doesn't offer much in the way of entertainment. I always find plenty to do, however. You will, too, if you show an interest in your surroundings. Most nights I'm worn out enough to go to sleep early."

Scarcely hearing what he said, she was trying to think of a way to reserve the lower bunk for herself.

"Do you want to go outside again tonight?" he asked.

"No, but I'm certainly capable of going by myself," she said.

"Not once I'm asleep, Gina. Then you're in for the night."

"I may need to go out later."

"Then you'll have to wake me to unlock the door."

Her voice caught in her throat. Was she going to be a true prisoner, locked in at night like a criminal?

"One of the keys I'm wearing opens this padlock," he said, taking a more-than-substantial-looking lock out of a metal box she hadn't noticed.

"You're locking me in?" She didn't want to believe it.

"I hope you're not foolish enough to start down the mountain in the dark, but for your own protection, I'm making sure you can't. The windows are too small to crawl through, and the door will be padlocked from the inside."

"What if there's a fire? It could be dangerous."

"I'll face that remote possibility if it happens. Our chances of getting out are better than your chance if you meet a grizzly. They're touchy animals at best. I always check the clearing before I go to bed," he said, pulling a long case from the floor under the bunks.

To her surprise and horror, he took out a wicked-looking rifle.

"Don't look so worried. I've never shot anything but a deer in season, and then only because I needed the meat to survive up here."

"You make it sound like you're here a lot."

"Every chance I get, but not nearly as much as I'd like. I dream of spending the winter here some year, maybe if Dad gets well enough to carry more of the responsibility again."

Completely unbidden, the thought came to her mind that Bruce should help his family too. Angry at herself, she pushed it aside quickly.

Her escape plan was greatly complicated by the padlock, but nevertheless she used Jon's brief absence to search some of the obvious places where he might have hidden the keys to the van. Her plans didn't include any encounters with bears, so finding them became much more urgent. First she checked the undersides of drawers and shelves, then she carefully stomped on floorboards looking for loose ones. Jonathan caught her doing that, his laugh irritating her more than a rebuke could have.

"You're not even warm, Gina. And in case you get any funny ideas about the rifle, I'm unloading it and locking the ammunition in my metal box along with all the available knives, wrenches, and other potential weapons. The key to the box stays on my neck chain too."

"Don't you have a ball and chain and ankle irons?" she asked bitterly. "Haven't you done enough, ruining my life and making Bruce think I deserted him?"

"I've hurt you more than I wanted to, but you will come out ahead, I promise you."

"I don't want your money," she cried out, perilously close to shedding tears of sheer rage.

"Please, don't tell me again how much you love my brother. I've been hearing that from women for years, my own mother included."

"You're jealous of your brother!"

43

"You may think you've drawn blood on that one, but you're still a long way off base. Let's go to bed, Gina."

"I'll take the lower bunk."

"Why?"

"I get dizzy in uppers."

"You can do better than that. Why not tell me you're afraid of falling off or upper bunks make your nose bleed? Not that it matters. You get the upper unless you want to share my bunk. That might complicate the matter of our annulment, of course, but either way, you'll wake me up if you try to sneak out of bed."

"You're terrible."

"I'm sure that you think so," he said wearily. "I'm afraid seventeen days are going to be a long haul."

His arrangements were simple; he'd brought two down-filled sleeping bags, one for each of them, but no sheets. At least he had several plump pillows and spare blankets.

"Tuck this blanket under the edge of the top mattress so it hangs down to make a little dressing room you can use to change for bed."

"I can sleep in my clothes."

"You won't be comfortable that way, and you must realize by now that sleeping is all you'll be doing tonight. Whatever plans you have to wander off, forget them. Even if you weren't locked in, you wouldn't make a mile in the dark, assuming you didn't provide a midnight snack for a bear. You'd better know, too, that I sleep in the nude, so give me a warning before you leave your bunk."

"You have everything planned very nicely, don't you? Nicely for you! How is Bruce going to take this when he learns what you've done?"

"My brother and I haven't had a fistfight in fifteen years, and we're too old to start one now. Also Bruce needs my good will more than I need his. My father wisely put the financial reins in my hands."

A dozen childish threats occurred to her, but she

44

choked them back. Seventeen days away from Bruce stretched ahead of her like an eternity, but somehow, some way, she would find an escape. Jon couldn't keep her under twenty-four-hour surveillance.

All her nightwear had been packed with a honeymoon in mind, but she did have one long gown in the peignoir set Claire had given her. She pulled it out of her suitcase, then found a serviceable blouse to button over it. It was a silly combination, but modest.

She could touch a rough-hewn beam from where she lay, and whenever she turned over, the bunk squeaked. The cabin's thick walls were a barrier against the wilderness, but night sounds came to her all too clearly through the tiny window Jon had swung outward on the far side of the room. She'd been right about one thing—his rhythmic breathing told her that he'd fallen asleep almost immediately.

A startling sound that she guessed was the hoot of an owl made her sit upright, nearly cracking her head on the low ceiling. How could she ever get to sleep knowing that Bruce was in a towering rage or a black depression because his bride-to-be had stood him up? Rolling over to the outer edge made the bunk creak so loudly she was sure Jon would wake up, but he didn't. Gradually she eased her way over the edge, a cautious process since the bunk wasn't equipped with a ladder. Standing absolutely motionless, she was grateful that he hadn't stirred.

Sprawled out across the mattress on his back, he seemed even larger than he did awake, dwarfing the roomy bunk. A woman would have to fight for space in his bed, Gina thought, quickly suppressing an image of herself squeezed in beside him. The moon was cooperating, filling the room with a faintly hazy glow, but the shadow of the upper bunk made Jon's bunk too dark to distinguish anything but the bulk of his body. She bent over him with extreme wariness, being careful not to touch the bed; his might squeak as easily as hers. The partly unzipped sleeping bag left his bare chest exposed to the night air, and it also gave her a better chance. With the lightest possible touch, she groped for the keys, shivering nervously when her fingers brushed over fine strands of curly hair.

When he stirred slightly, she had to retreat, but his even breathing gave her the go-ahead sign again. This time she located the keys easily, but the problem came in removing them from the chain. The metallic rope wouldn't separate when she tried to pull it apart, and if there was a clasp, he was sleeping on top of it.

Gingerly, holding her breath and moving very, very slowly, she was able to raise the chain over his head without catching it in his hair. At that point she was stymied. The only way to free it from the back of his neck was to tug vigorously, hoping he wouldn't wake up. It was a very slim chance. Fear of what he would do if she woke him made her pause, and her hesitation paid off. He turned in his sleep, lying on his side and facing the door so the chain fell freely down the side of the pillow.

Slipping her bare feet into the cold interiors of her shoes was unpleasant, but she barely noticed, so anxious was she to carry out her plan. What she hadn't expected was that the lock would groan in protest when she tried first one key, then the other. Actually opening it was even noisier, and she was prepared to dash out the door when she heard another slight sound.

"What do you intend to do now?"

Jon's hand shot out and covered her cold fingers still clasping the lock.

"You have no right to keep me prisoner," she said, trembling with anger and disappointment.

"I warned you, Gina. I'm a light sleeper, no matter how tired I am. Were you going to try walking out of here tonight?"

"Of course not," she snapped. "I just resent being locked in at night like a jailbird."

"So you were going to get rid of my lock?"

There was no answer to that.

"It wouldn't matter, Gina. Lock or no lock, you can't leave at night without my hearing. If it makes you worry less about fire, I'll leave it off at night. You won't have to worry about getting out in an emergency, but from now on you're spreading your sleeping bag between the wall and me."

He took the heavy metal lock from her hand, and the moonlight played eerie tricks with his features, softening them, giving them the dreamy look Bruce had before he kissed her.

She couldn't help being aware that the man beside her was stark naked, his shoulder muscles gleaming in the moon-washed dimness. For a crazy moment she wanted to touch him, then a stab of renewed anger made her back away. She tried to take the lock back, but his free hand snaked out and captured her wrist, making the heavy metal object drop to the floor.

"You can't win this war," he said. "The best you can hope for is an honorable peace."

"How can you use the word *honorable* when you've stolen your brother's wife?"

"Gina, Bruce isn't going to welcome you back waving a marriage license." His voice was gentle now, intensely persuasive. "Believe me, and you'll save yourself a lot of pain."

"He'll know this wasn't my fault."

"It won't matter. Bruce will never marry you. If you won't accept that, you'll suffer much more."

"You don't care if I suffer! You've made a shambles of my life!"

"How old are you? Twenty-two?"

47

"Twenty-four. Didn't you read the marriage license application? But my age has nothing to do with this."

"It does. You're young and you'll heal. I speak from experience."

Something in his voice stirred her compassion, but she didn't want to feel anything but hatred for this man who'd deceived her so cruelly.

"Get your sleeping bag and pillow," he ordered in an entirely different voice.

"You can't expect me to sleep with you."

"You're my wife, aren't you?" he taunted her. "But no, I expect you to sleep beside me, not with me. I want a trouble-free annulment."

"I won't do it."

"A showdown so soon?" It unnerved her that he actually laughed, a deep sound that matched the sleekly muscled body she was trying hard not to see. "Dearest wife, I can make you do anything I like, but caveman tactics aren't my style."

His grip on her arm was firm but not painful, yet she had no doubts that his powerful fingers could cause excruciating pain if he willed it.

"At least put on some clothes!" she admonished him, not conceding total defeat.

"That's a reasonable request, I guess."

He dropped her arm and went to the drawer where he'd put his clothing. She kept her head turned away until he spoke again.

"That's all the concession you'll get. Clothes are too binding for sleep."

His shorts stood out whitely in the dark room, but her small victory didn't raise her spirits. She watched dejectedly as he pulled down her pillow and sleeping bag and threw them on his mattress.

"Crawl in," he ordered, moving toward her when she didn't move.

So close to the wall that her arm would scrape against a rough log if she moved, she tried to sleep without success. She was trapped, his body as unyielding a barrier as the thick wall. Only by making herself as small as possible could she avoid contact with his outstretched arm or bulky sleeping bag. Her situation was intolerable. How could she make him listen to reason and take her back to civilization? Dozens of pleas and arguments raced through her mind, but there wasn't one with any chance of success.

He moaned in his sleep then, shifting his whole body closer to her, his fingers lightly brushing her cheek. Angrily she pushed his arm away, not caring if she woke him or not. Even exposed to the night air, his arm felt warm, and she kept her hand on it a moment longer than necessary. This should have been Bruce beside her, holding her against him, cherishing her, teaching her the mysteries of love. Never, never, never would she forgive the man who'd stolen that from her.

CHAPTER THREE

She was dancing, caught up in the arms of the man she loved, his Navy dress whites sparkling against the deep tan of his face, his warm brown eyes so compelling that she felt herself go limp with longing. His mouth met hers, teasing and begging that she surrender her soft pink lips, making her whole body tingle with desire. Shuddering, she pressed closer, but her urgency was replaced by vague anxieties. She captured one strand of soft, black hair falling across his forehead, but under her gaze it coarsened, becoming wiry and abrasive to her touch.

His cheek was bristly as she trailed the sensitive backs of her fingers across his scratchy jaw. Suddenly the vision of her dreams merged with the very real face beside her, and all the pain returned. The eyes that opened to stare piercingly into hers weren't those of her beloved Bruce, and she jerked her hand away as though seared by burning coals.

She wanted to die of embarrassment. In her sleep she had been fondling the face of the man she hated.

He propped himself up on one elbow, eyeing her with a mixture of curiosity and skepticism.

"What was that about?"

"I was dreaming," she explained lamely.

"About my brother, I assume."

"Of course!"

"Nothing you can do will get you off this mountain any sooner, Gina, and nothing is going to interfere with our annulment."

"I didn't mean to touch you!" she cried out, humiliated by his insinuation. "Remember, it was your idea to make me sleep here. I'm not used to sleeping with only six inches of space."

"You wouldn't have to sleep beside me if I could trust you not to expose yourself to danger by trying to get through the woods at night. I'm serious about this, Gina. Even if you follow the road, you can't make it on foot. Do you have any idea how far we drove without passing anything, not a house or store or gas station?"

She shook her head, still hating herself for having unintentionally touched him.

"An experienced hiker would make at least a two-day trip of it, and he'd carry food, water, a sleeping bag, a first-aid kit, flashlight, and insect repellent, not to mention some items for personal comfort. The mosquitoes are more vicious than the bears."

"Just take me home," she begged, hating the pleading tone in her voice.

"I'll see that you get wherever you want to go in sixteen days, provided, of course, that you agree in writing to the annulment. My lawyer drew up a perfectly legal document."

"You took time to see a lawyer? How long did you plan this kidnapping?"

"Honeymoon," he corrected her ruefully, sitting upright now and exposing his chest to the morning chill. "The first two days Bruce was home I used every possible argument to persuade him to postpone the wedding, but logic and common sense don't appeal to my brother. When he refused to invite you to visit the family before the wedding, he left me no choice. I made my own plans. Bruce is always jotting down reminders to himself, then mislaying them, so I found your parents' names that way, not to mention the arrival time of your plane."

"You snooped in your brother's personal things? The more I find out about you, the more I can't believe you're Bruce's twin. He would never do a thing like that to you."

"You seemed to like the two-days growth on my chin, though."

"Oh! Get away from me!"

Impulsively she swung her pillow at his head, connecting squarely in his face. He sprang on top of her, pinning her hands above her head and stirring a memory of something she'd forgotten in her anger. In the diner parking lot she'd awakened with her head on Jon's shoulder, and he hadn't been indifferent to her then. He'd kissed her aggressively, heatedly, arousing them both to a fever-pitch before he broke off abruptly. She felt as though he'd just handed her a new weapon in her struggle to get back to Bruce. Walking off the mountain seemed almost impossible, but there was a way to make Jon take her back. What he wanted was a neat, convenient annulment, not a messy, expensive divorce. Would he be so willing to be her jailer if his own desires threatened his plan?

Did she dare play games with him? A nervous tremor ran down her spine, as she realized how dangerous an opponent he was, but desperation made her bold. She flicked her tongue over her full lower lip, squirming but not trying to escape his grip.

"Make this easier for both of us, Gina. Promise me you won't risk your life wandering out of the cabin at night, and you can sleep wherever you choose."

"And if I choose right here?" she asked, feeling slightly ridiculous but hoping her voice sounded provocative.

"I'll use the upper bunk."

His words were casual enough, but there was a catch in his voice revealing that his calmness was partly a pose. For a moment she pretended he was Bruce, almost convincing herself that she wanted him to kiss her.

"Sharing a bunk could be interesting," she whispered.

"You little witch!" he said scornfully. "Have you decided that one Kenyon husband is as convenient as the other?"

He'd sensed her trap but misinterpreted her reason, and the anger that flooded her was so intense she thought she'd explode. Kicking and squirming, she slipped free of his grasp.

"Get away from me!" she cried.

"Gladly, since you've decided to do everything the hard way," he said, sliding off the mattress.

Burying her head in a pillow didn't completely muffle the sounds he made padding around barefooted in the confined space of the cabin. His presence, angry and noisy, filled the room even when she tried to shut it out by pressing both hands against her ears. When she looked up again, the room was quiet, and he was standing by the door wearing a navy terry cloth robe and rubber thongs.

"If you want a bath," he said coldly, "be outside in two minutes. You're not going alone, and this is your one chance today."

She started to ask questions about his offer, but he slammed the door managing a much more satisfactory bang than she had the previous day.

"Damn, damn, damn," she said aloud, so angry that she wanted to throw something.

She felt grubby and beat and so out-of-sorts she didn't even recognize herself. After wasting half a minute dreading any further contact with her jailer, she decided that a bath was probably the best thing that would happen to her that day. It took her considerably longer than the time he'd allotted to find her own terry robe and some sandals she'd planned to wear walking to and from a luxurious Las Vegas pool. Her cosmetic bag held shampoo and other beauty aids, but no soap. It had never occurred to her that she wouldn't be showering in a well-stocked motel room. After stripping, she slipped into the robe and tied it securely. She had no intention of really jeopardizing the annulment. Even in her anger she recognized the danger in challenging Jon's self-restraint.

Too upset to come up with any workable solution to her problems, she stormed out the door, and, as she'd anticipated, he was still waiting, shivering slightly in the chill September air.

"I like an early morning dip," he commented.

"That stream must be like ice."

"No one's forcing you to go in," he said indifferently.

The air was so chilly she looked for frost on the ground, and she found herself following Jon's lead, running just to keep warm.

Standing beside the stream with goose bumps forming on her arms and thighs, Gina had strong second thoughts. Only a polar bear could comfortably jump into the frigid current without a wet suit.

"I don't have a towel or soap or a washcloth," she alibied. "I'll go back to get them."

"No need. I'm the perfect host."

He unfolded the bundle he was carrying and handed her all three items, squelching her excuse for not going into the water.

"You first," she said, wondering if she had enough courage to take off her robe when he was so near.

"There won't be any turns. The name of the game is speed. We both hit the water together."

"Not on your life!"

"You have a choice, upstream or downstream. No peeking, scout's honor."

54

"I'll never take the word of a man who impersonates his brother."

"Are you backing out or not? I don't intend to stand here playing games."

"I'm not. I'll go upstream."

"Go downstream on the other side of that boulder. The current won't be as swift, and your modesty will be preserved."

He was right, of course. The huge rock made a secluded little spot for bathing, but she was too agitated to thank him for pointing it out. Gingerly she edged her way toward the boulder that almost touched the shoreline. After she dropped her robe, she doubted that she had enough nerve to plunge into the water. With soap in one hand and the cloth in the other, she dipped one toe into the swiftly flowing water; it was so cold it hurt.

The best she could tolerate was a quick sponge bath standing on the edge of the stream. She tried to work up some suds, but the soap didn't lather well in the icy water. By the time she'd washed her face, her whole body felt raw and abused from the brisk wind.

"Oh, darn," she said dejectedly.

Maybe if she caught pneumonia, her husband-in-name-only would rush her off the mountain to a hospital. The risk would be worth it if she could get back to Bruce and explain what had happened. Recklessly she plunged in and was almost paralyzed by the shock. The water was only thigh-high, but it slapped against her exposed backside and made her shiver uncontrollably. Deciding she couldn't be any more miserable, she ducked down, immersing her body up to her neck. The water-smoothed stones underfoot were uncomfortable on her feet and slippery, and her frantic leap for shore turned into a minor disaster. She slipped backward and went under the water.

Basically unhurt except for a few minor bruises, she pulled herself out of the stream and managed to force her arms into the sleeves of her robe. Her feet got gritty before she found her sandals, and her wet hair streamed over her face, partly blinding her.

"Hurry up, Gina," Jon's voice called out to her from upstream.

With shaky hands she wrapped the thick towel around her head and stumbled away from the stream. Never, never again would she expose her body to the punishing, bone-chilling water in that stream.

"Enjoy it?" he asked, falling into step beside her.

He looked as wet as she was, but she couldn't believe he'd come out of it smiling.

"You knew what it would be like," she accused him darkly.

"Better than a cold shower for cooling things down."

She broke into a run, spurred on by his soft laughter. From now on it would be total, unrestrained warfare between them. Let him gloat over the success of his plan to thwart the marriage. She had all kinds of weapons in her arsenal, and this unspeakable man wasn't going to have the last laugh.

She only wished he didn't look exactly like the man she loved.

"I'll light the stove while you use our dressing facilities," he said when he came into the cabin a few seconds behind her. "You're so cold you're shaking."

His consideration only made her more agitated, and she fumbled around awkwardly, picking out underwear, jeans, and a pullover top. Deliberately she dressed as slowly as possible behind the blanket, stalling not because it accomplished anything, but because it gave her the only bit of privacy possible in the cabin. She needed time to regain her composure and decide what to do next. She felt as though they were playing a complicated game, and she didn't know the rules.

56

Jon was dressed himself by the time she finished, and the stove was radiating heat that felt heaven-sent.

"I left most of our food supplies in the van," he said. "They're as secure there as anywhere, and it stays pretty cool in the clearing, even on warm days. When the water on the stove boils, you make coffee. I'll go get some things for breakfast."

"You're trusting me out of your sight?"

"Yes, but not out of hearing. Sound carries well up here. Oh, I left two drawers empty for whatever you want to unpack."

"I don't want to unpack anything," she said, allowing herself the luxury of a little self-pity. "What does a prisoner need besides cloth shoes and a toothbrush?"

"Play it your way then," he said, seemingly unruffled.

Even if she'd wanted to make coffee, she didn't have the slightest idea how to go about it without an automatic coffee maker. She doubted if throwing coarse grounds from the tin container on the table into the water would result in very good coffee, but she declined to experiment, feeling overwhelmed by everything that had happened. When he returned in a few minutes, the water was boiling furiously in a big aluminum kettle on the stove, but Gina was propped up on pillows trying unsuccessfully to become interested in one of the paperbacks he'd brought.

"Coffee ready?" he asked.

"No."

"If you don't know how to make it, I'd better give you some lessons."

"That won't be necessary." She didn't look up from the book, even though her absorption in the printed page was only a ruse.

"I know being here wasn't your idea, but the time will pass much more pleasantly if we work at it. It doesn't matter to me, but if you help out with the chores, it will give you something to do."

"You're my jailer, not my camping buddy!" she cried out defensively. "How can you talk about making coffee and doing chores when you're ruining my life?"

"That remains to be proven. I could be doing you a favor."

"You must hate your brother."

"No, but I can't approve of the way he uses people. I'm only trying to save his share of our family's holdings. Bruce likes to spend money, huge sums of money. He'll thank me someday for helping him avoid another large community property settlement."

"You keep assuming our marriage wouldn't work. I only plan to marry once. I'll make my marriage work."

"I sincerely hope you're not making plans to celebrate our golden anniversary."

"Our marriage is nothing but a bad dream. You're a criminal, keeping me here against my will."

"Maybe, but we're still going to be here until I'm sure Bruce is at sea. I hope you won't make it any harder on yourself than necessary."

She turned her attention back to the book without answering him, forcing herself to make some sense of the words that seemed to swim on the page. When he sat down on the edge of the bunk, she turned the unread page, trying to ignore him without success.

"Look at me," he said softly.

She wanted to refuse, but there was a compelling quality in his voice that weakened her resistance. Thinking about his deceitfulness, she armed herself with anger so she could overlook his almost uncanny resemblance to Bruce and treat him as the enemy he was.

"You're not what I expected," he said, sounding puzzled, "and I'll try to make your stay here as free of unpleasantness as possible, but you have to meet me halfway."

"What do you expect? My marriage is a mockery and

the man I love thinks I deserted him. You've got to take me back to Las Vegas before Bruce leaves."

"I'll fix breakfast," he said as though he hadn't heard her.

"You just can't keep me here against my will," she went on desperately. "There must be laws against this kind of thing. If you don't care about Bruce, what about your parents? Will it help your father's health to know that you're a fraud and a kidnapper?"

"My father isn't going to know. You won't tell him."

"You're incredible! You can't force me to be quiet about this. You've done a terrible thing."

"A necessary thing, and it only concerns three people, you, me, and Bruce. Aside from my lawyer, who's also my best friend, we're the only ones who will know. It's in the annulment agreement, along with the amount of the settlement. You'll find it's a generous one, but you won't get a lump sum. To receive all the payments, you have to maintain absolute silence about the circumstances of our marriage and annulment."

"I'll never agree to do that, and I won't accept a precious cent of yours."

"Then you'll be making a costly and foolish mistake. You stand to lose a great deal if you don't follow my rules."

"You have the most unbelievable gall. How can you lay down rules for me after the mean, conniving trick you played to get me here?"

"There have to be rules in any situation. Right now I hold all the cards. If you want to do things the hard way, it's your decision."

Sixteen days, she thought morosely as she sat on the bed watching him fry bacon, then crack several eggs into the hot drippings. She wanted to throw his breakfast in his face, but common sense won out. One way or another, she was leaving, and she needed her strength.

59

"Come and get it," he said, after a remarkably short time spent in preparation.

The bacon was deliciously crisp, the eggs were sunny-side up, crackly around the edges, and the whole wheat bread was sliced thick and dripping honey, but everything was tasteless to her. She ate because she was hungry, but it was an effort to swallow.

"If you're reasonable, you might find my retreat a pleasant place," he said, when both of them had finished.

"Nothing about being here is reasonable. You married me by fraud, brought me here against my will, and tried to make me believe lies about the man I love. I want to leave now. Now, Mr. Kenyon."

"Call me Jon," he said, getting up from the table. "And let me know if you need more water. I'll help you carry some from the stream. There's enough left to wash up these dishes, though."

The prospect of sitting with nothing to do was so dreary she glanced around the cabin for some diversion. His presence seemed suffocating, and every hour they spent together was going to be a trial. She sat at the table nursing the last of the cold tea in her cup for a long time, feeling nauseated by the bits of bacon fat congealing on her plate. Fidgeting with the dull-bladed table knife, she tried to think of some plan, any plan, that would force him to take her back to Las Vegas. Her life really would be ruined if Bruce sailed without knowing that she'd been tricked into not meeting him. Idly she ran the blade across her wrist, but she wasn't quite foolish enough to fake a suicide attempt, not that the knife was sharp enough anyway.

What if she swallowed some plant outside and pretended that she was poisoned? Would Jon rush her to the nearest hospital where she could find help getting away from him? It was the best idea she'd had so far, but, of course, she had to reject it. She didn't know a thing about wild plants, and a random choice might make her really ill. Also his first-aid kit, prominently placed in the metal cabinet, might contain all sorts of unpleasant remedies for accidental poisoning.

If he was counting on an annulment, why had he kissed her so thoroughly when they stopped at the diner? Had it been part of his ruse, a ploy to quiet her suspicions until they reached the cabin? That seemed unlikely. By then they'd been well on their way; he didn't need to be as convincing as he had before the wedding. No, he had enjoyed kissing her. If he wanted her enough, his plan for an annulment would be endangered, and he would have to take her back to civilization. But there were too many flaws in any plan to tempt him. Even if she had enough confidence to try to seduce any man, she couldn't be sure how it would end. She wanted the annulment even more than he did. Also she was so angry that just being civil was an effort. She wasn't a good enough actress to make herself seem appealing when she was so upset. There just didn't seem to be any way to induce him to take her back.

"Still thinking about how you'll get away?" he asked, kneeling beside the metal chest that he kept securely locked. "Believe me, it's a waste of effort to try, Gina."

Startled that he seemed to have read her mind, she reacted angrily. "I'm a prisoner here against my will, and I must leave."

"Gina, your stubbornness will only get you into trouble. You can't leave here until I let you."

His cheerful tone infuriated her, and, what was worse, he was right in a way. Stubbornness had led her into his trap. She had refused to listen to the urgent warnings of her family, her roommate, even her employer. A week probably wasn't long enough to know a man before making such a crucial decision. She should have suggested that she visit Bruce's family and spend time becoming better acquainted with him. A less impulsive course would have given her an opportunity to meet Bruce's twin and would have saved her from the impossible situation she was in.

Restless, she got up and paced the cabin, but the small amount of floor space didn't allow her very spirited exercise. Jon was still on his knees, relocking the box, but beside him on the floor was a large pad of paper and artist's charcoal.

"I hope to sketch some wildlife," he said conversationally. "You might enjoy coming along with me. There are a lot of things to see in the woods if you know what to look for."

"No."

"I hate to leave you locked in here alone all morning," he protested mildly, "but it's your choice. Would you like to help me get water before I leave?"

"No."

"Suit yourself. If you change your mind, call out the window. I won't be far away."

He gathered up all the food remnants to take with him, explaining that all he was storing in the cabin was canned goods. After giving her one more chance to come with him, he left, noisily securing the door from the outside.

Besides the dishes, she found a few minor jobs to do. Both sleeping bags needed to be rolled up and stowed for the day, and the scattered pillows gave an unmade look to the room. His damp robe was hanging on a wall hook, as were his towel and washcloth, but hers were wadded in a corner of the bed. But even the tedious job of doing dishes in a pan with water heated on the stove didn't take very long, and the morning stretched ahead like an eternity. She alternated her time between angry pacing and searching in every conceivable spot for the keys to the van.

Finally she dropped to the bed, totally defeated, but soon got up again to unzip and spread out one of the sleeping bags like a bedspread; the plastic mattress covering was sticky-feeling on her bare arms. It was a futile gesture; she was much too agitated to relax on the bed, let alone sleep on it.

As exits the windows were hopelessly small, rationing the light that flowed into the cabin, but she could use them as peepholes by standing on a chair. She was able to see most of the clearing on three sides, but she didn't see Jon. After what seemed like a hundred hours, noon finally came, but he didn't return for lunch. It was nearly one thirty by her watch before he came into the cabin.

"Hungry?" he asked conversationally, filling the cabin with his presence. A fresh, woody scent clung to his clothes, and his face was slightly flushed, as though he'd been out in the wind.

"No," she said quickly, then realized it wasn't true.

"Maybe some exercise will make you as hungry as I am."

His idea of exercise was to insist that she pace around the clearing while he leaned his back against a tree trunk, seemingly preoccupied with his sketch pad but ready to call her back if she started to wander in the direction of the van. After half an hour or so, he left to bring up some supplies from the van for a cold lunch.

She spent a long afternoon broken only by one crying jag and a fitful nap. She made tea and let it sit forgotten until it was cold, then reheated it just to do something. Matches were kept in an old-fashioned painted tin holder on the wall, and an ample supply of wood was piled beside the stove. Her boredom was getting so unbearable she toyed with the idea of setting the cabin on fire, but quickly rejected it as another foolish fantasy. For a while she entertained herself by lighting wooden matches one at a time and letting each burn down to a small bit of stick before she blew it out. She knew it was childish, but it was something to do.

He came in quietly, watching her from the doorway until she blew out her match. Faintly embarrassed at having been caught, she avoided looking at his face, but the object in his hand caught her eye. It was a substantial-sized fish, which he slapped down on the table, taking a sharp knife from his locked box and going about the business of cleaning it, using the last of the water in the bucket.

"You can eat fresh-water fish, can't you?"

"Yes," she said, aware of the hollowness in her stomach.

"I've had time to think," he said quietly.

"And?"

"It doesn't matter whether I lock you in or not."

"It certainly does," she said, knowing that she shouldn't push her luck but needing an outlet for all her rage and disappointment. "You know Bruce is going to hear about everything that you've done to me."

"Don't make silly threats, Gina."

His voice was so low that she spoke more quietly herself.

"Does this mean you've decided not to keep me prisoner?"

"You're not a prisoner. You're a frightened, disappointed young woman, and whether you believe it or not, I'm not proud of what I've done. I still think it was the only way to deal with another of Bruce's foolish infatuations, but I don't like myself very much at this point."

"Bruce loves me," she insisted, hating the demeaning word he'd used to describe her fiancé's feelings. He made it sound as if his brother had a school-boy crush on her. "I don't care what you think of me or what you do to me, Jonathan, but don't belittle my relationship with Bruce. You have no right to do that."

The seriousness in her voice made him stare searchingly into her face.

"No, I don't," he agreed.

He picked up two of the pails he used for hauling water

64

and walked out of the cabin, not bothering to lock the door behind him.

For a brief instant she saw the open doorway as the pathway to freedom, stepping outside to stare at the tall trees that marked the route to the van. But, of course, nothing had changed. She might get down to the clearing before Jon returned, but she couldn't drive the van without keys. Worse, she believed him about the dangers of trying to hike out alone. In her whole life, her only contact with the wilderness had been a guided tour of the Wisconsin Dells. Even if the trip was an easy one for an experienced hiker, she didn't have the skills or knowledge to attempt it alone. Also Jon would undoubtedly be true to his word and follow her, and no doubt he'd catch her too. Being brought back in chains, so to speak, was more humiliation than she could endure at the moment. She would escape and soon, but she had to have a plan with some chance of success. Running off empty-handed while he fetched water was sheer foolishness. She went back into the cabin so he wouldn't suspect that she'd been tempted to flee.

When he returned, he went to work silently, heating water, and getting things ready for dinner. In her boredom she really would have liked to help him; her pride made her hold back, but any activity would have been better than the enforced idleness that left her a victim of her unhappy thoughts. A hundred times she'd imagined the scene when Bruce met her plane and she wasn't on it. Had he waited for the next flight or made calls immediately? Knowing his natural impatience, he probably had her mother on the phone within minutes. How cruel that her whole future could be shattered in such a short time.

The smell of mountain trout frying over a wood fire did enticing things to Gina's appetite, and for a little while she worried that Jon wouldn't invite her to share it with him, so absolute was his power over her. He did, of course, calling her to the table so casually that they might have been camping buddies after all.

"It's delicious," she commented, breaking a silence that had lasted through most of the meal.

"Thank you, but the fish deserves most of the credit."

He cleaned up without asking for her help, and she was left with nothing to do but watch him. He still hadn't shaved, and the dark bristles on his face gave him a slightly sinister look. She hoped he would grow a beard, anything to change his almost uncanny resemblance to Bruce. It was so easy to watch Jon and see his twin. Not only were their faces identical, sharply etched with sensual lips and straight white teeth, even their eyebrows and ears seemed the same. Gina loved Bruce's strong chin line and his slightly hollowed cheeks that invited her caress. It was maddening to see the same features on a man she detested.

Jon bent over the iron monster of a stove, scrubbing off particles of grease that had splashed out of the frying pan. He'd cast aside his shirt to work over the still-hot stove, and the dim light of a kerosene lantern played over the muscled expanse of his back. She loved the way his waist tapered narrowly to firm buttocks and long, powerful legs. Except when he moved with a very slight stiffness in one leg, she might have been watching Bruce.

Because Jon neither spoke nor turned toward her, she was able to enjoy the illusion that he was Bruce, her husband and lover who would soon come to her. The urge to put her arms around him and caress his firm torso was almost overpowering, and she felt a shiver of longing course down her spine.

For the first time in two days she wondered how she looked. Certainly the icy dunking hadn't been a satisfactory substitute for a real shampoo, and her naturally wavy hair felt tangled to her touch. She knew her attractiveness didn't depend on cosmetics, but still she longed for a touch of eye makeup and lipstick to make her feel more like herself.

"Can I wash my hair?" she finally asked hesitantly.

"All right," he agreed after a long pause. "I'll mix some hot and cold water in a kettle, and you can wash it over a pan."

He made the arrangements efficiently, but indicated that she had to use the same towel she'd used that morning.

"We'll only do laundry once a week," he said.

She didn't want to think about being there a full week, let alone fifteen more days, but she was glad she'd hung up her towel. The stove made the cabin so warm that it was nearly dry.

After thoroughly brushing it, she dampened her hair by cupping water in her hands, letting the drops splash into the pan. She used the shampoo sparingly, realizing that rinse water was limited, but she worked it in well, enjoying not only the cleansing but the activity. A full day of idleness had left her longing for something useful to do.

Even though Jon was stretched out on the bottom bunk, she sensed his eyes following her movement. Given the size and closeness of the cabin, she could hardly demand that he hide his face while she washed her hair, but his gaze was disquieting. Bruce loved to bury his face in her hair, teasing it around his fingers, making a sensual act of an innocent caress.

"Let me help you rinse it."

"What?" Gina gave a nervous start.

"It will be easier for me to pour the rinse water. Save me having to dry off the floor."

"I'll clean up after myself."

"No trouble."

He reached the kettle of water before she could protest, standing over her as she needlessly spent more time working the suds between her fingers.

"Bend over the pan when you're ready," he said.

"Oh, all right," she agreed uncomfortably.

Leaning over the pan she felt foolish and vulnerable, but when Jon slipped one hand over her forehead to shield her eyes, she experienced an entirely different sensation. He let the pleasantly warm water dribble slowly over her scalp, trying to rinse away the suds with the least possible amount of water. Warm currents tingled all the way down her back as he used the last of the water and put the kettle aside, squeezing away excess water with surprising gentleness. She groped for her towel, but he was too quick, reaching it first and wrapping it around her head, using one corner to wipe stray drops from her forehead.

"Put your head against my chest," he ordered.

"No," she protested, but he pulled her head forward, absorbing water with the towel while he caused the most delicious feeling to race through her scalp.

"That's enough," she protested again, pushing at his chest with two damp hands, then pulling them away quickly when her palms felt stung by the wiry silkiness of the hairs on his torso.

"Want me to brush it?" he asked lightly, not completely concealing an undercurrent of new feeling in his voice.

"No, thank you."

She hurried as far from him as possible, leaving him with the damp towel in his hands, and attacked her hair with a brush, punishing each strand for putting her in a position where she felt something for her captor.

"When you're done, it's my turn."

"What?" The tone of his voice startled her.

"That stream isn't meant for shampooing. You can do the honors for me when you're done brushing."

Her defenses down, she still tried to challenge him.

"Who does your hair when you don't have a kidnap victim with you?"

"I don't need to resort to kidnapping for female atten-

68

tion, but since you've enjoyed my services, turnabout is only fair."

"Nothing about my being here is fair."

"Maybe not, but you owe me a shampoo."

"Only a rinse."

"Yes, let's keep things even."

She didn't want to watch him as he leaned over the pan to dampen his hair, but her eyes were fickle allies. The outline of his spine stood out as he angled his long body over the pan, and his jeans slipped slightly, revealing a ribbon of lighter skin below his sun-bronzed back. For a fleeting instant she could imagine running her finger down the ridges of his back, but sanity returned quickly.

Turning toward her, he lathered his head, forcing her to avert her eyes. Even in the dim light of late evening, she couldn't be comfortable with her awareness of him.

"I'm ready."

His voice pulled her back from a far distance.

"The rinse you owe me. I've mixed the water."

Touching him wasn't a good idea. Every atom of her being warned her against it, yet pouring water was a simple enough act. She did it hurriedly, not considerately sheltering his eyes as he had done for her. The water swooshed over his sudsy hair, flooding his ears and bringing an oath when the soap stung his eyes.

"You're supposed to close your eyes," she said, chiding him to conceal her own agitation.

He groped for his towel and rubbed his eyes while water streamed down his torso.

"You're a fiend," he accused her.

"I'm sorry. I'm not used to shampooing men."

"Dry my hair," he ordered.

"You can dry it yourself."

She retreated, but not quickly enough. He grabbed her arm, pulling her so close that the front of her sweater picked up damp stains from his chest.

"You owe me."

"I can't even reach your head."

"I'll sit," he said grabbing a wooden chair away from the table and thrusting his towel into her hands.

She was playing a losing game; all the chips were in his pile. With a reluctance that had nothing to do with drying his hair, she approached him, rubbing his scalp at arm's length.

"Like this," he said pulling her closer and pressing his head against her midriff.

Her breath caught in her lungs, but not because of the impact of his head. She was trapped; the only way to avoid drying his hair was to admit that touching him affected her. How she hated this man whose appearance was a replica of Bruce's!

She massaged his scalp halfheartedly and stopped after only a few moments, knowing full well that his thick hair was far from dry. Trying to regain her composure, she helped him clean up, hanging both towels on their hooks.

"There's not much to do at night except go to bed," he said, "unless you play gin rummy."

"I do, but I don't want to play with you."

"Okay, if that's the way you feel." He sounded more amused than disappointed.

Bedtime was a repetition of the previous night until it came time to spread out their sleeping bags.

"Can I have your promise you won't try to walk down the mountain?" he asked.

"You can't have my promise about anything. You stole the only promises that mean anything, to love and cherish and . . ."

"Obey?"

"Stolen promises are worthless."

He walked to the bunks and threw the upper mattress onto the floor with a thrust that sent dust particles whirling in the circle of light made by the lantern.

"What are you doing?" she asked.

"I'm not going to lie there and let you play knick-knack on my nose all night."

"That was an accident. I was dreaming."

"About my brother, I hope."

"Certainly not about you. I despise you."

"Sure," he said indifferently, kicking the mattress against the door. "Well, it'd be a damn sight more comfortable if I could trust you, but you leave me no choice. The only way out this door is over my body, and you learned last night that I'm a very light sleeper."

What she hated most about sleeping in the same room with him, Gina decided hours later, was that he fell asleep so fast. Lying on her mattress and listening to the contented sound of his deep breathing was one more torture added to what had been the longest day of her life.

CHAPTER FOUR

The sound of the mattress being pulled across the floor roused her, and she sat up quickly, startled by her surroundings until all the events of the past two days flooded into her consciousness.

"Sorry I woke you," Jon said, lifting the mattress and sliding it back on the top bunk.

His terry robe was long, well below his knees, and tightly knotted, but she turned away anyway to avoid the feeling of intimacy his nearness caused.

"Do you want a bath in the stream?" he asked.

Even if the water in it had been steamy warm, she would have refused. Her restless night had made her decide to keep a wall between herself and Jon. In this isolated place, fully at his mercy, she didn't want her feelings for Bruce confused by the proximity of his twin. A cold, remote attitude seemed her best defense until she could find a way back to her fiancé, if she still had a fiancé. Would Bruce want to marry her after this disastrous false wedding? She pushed her doubts aside impatiently. Their love was so strong that someday they would laugh together over Jon's devious plan.

"I'll take a sponge bath here in the cabin," she said.

"All right. There's plenty of hot water on the stove. I'll knock before I come in."

Tempted as she was to stay huddled in the sleeping bag after he left, she forced herself to get up and hurry through a morning routine that included a tepid sponge bath instead of the longed-for soak in a hot tub. Most of the clothes she'd packed for her honeymoon were wholly impractical for cabin living, so she put on her only clean pair of jeans, topping them with a long-sleeved pale peach blouse that was too dressy but would have to serve. Doing laundry once a week wasn't going to stretch her supply of practical clothes far enough, but it wasn't regret for the lost honeymoon that oppressed her. She felt so out-of-control; her own destiny was being decided, and there was nothing she could do to alter it. The need to see and talk with Bruce was growing, not decreasing, and she desperately tried to think of some way to get to him.

Jon returned, and she went outside so he could dress. Dreading another day alone in the cabin with her thoughts, she fell into his routine without much conversation, helping him bring up food stored in the van for their breakfast.

"I'm going to cut some firewood to dry for next season," he said when breakfast was cleared away. "I saw a tree I want to cut not too far from here. If you want to come along while I chop wood, you're welcome."

"I suppose it's better than being locked in here all day."

"I said I wouldn't lock you in during the day. You can't get away anyway, but you'll save us both a lot of trouble if you don't try."

He walked over to the assortment of clothing hanging on wall pegs and took a wool plaid shirt, its collar and cuffs frayed but the deep greens and blues of the fabric still vivid.

"Here, wear this. You'll ruin your blouse in the woods."

Reluctantly she pulled the heavy shirt over her silk blouse and folded up the too-long sleeves. The wool had captured a faint scent of its owner, a musky, woodsy smell that was noticeable but not unpleasant. Gina stalked outside impatiently, letting the sharper scent of the pines clear her nostrils.

Jon led the way to the van where he armed himself with a formidable long-handled ax.

"Unfortunately it's downhill, so the wood will have to be hauled uphill," he said in a light tone that plainly told her he enjoyed the challenge.

The morning air was briskly cool, making her appreciate the warmth of the woolen shirt. She hurried to keep up with Jon, but several times he turned around and offered her his hand on a steep descent. Moving easily through the pathless woods in spite of his stiff leg, he looked like a logger, his red plaid shirt and heavy, laced boots completing the picture.

The trees were growing close together here, and the one he pointed out was something of a runt compared to the two giants flanking it.

"I'm going to take this one out. The safest place for you to stand is over there," he said, pointing with the ax.

"Couldn't you find one closer to the cabin?" she asked, not quite able to visualize how the towering trunk would end up in little pieces suitable for the stove.

"Probably, but I like to thin the crowded areas. You can tell by the skimpy branches that they're too thick here."

To her city-bred habit of thought, it seemed a shame to cut down a beautiful, thick-trunked tree just to burn it, but she didn't say so. They were playing by his rules, and she was the first to admit she knew nothing about living in the wilderness.

"Why did you build a cabin here?" she asked, voicing her curiosity.

"I was looking over property to invest in timber. I just

fell in love with this area, so I bought some land and built my cabin."

"Your family doesn't own this?"

"No, in fact," he said tossing his shirt on a low branch as he stripped down to a navy T-shirt, "Bruce doesn't even know I own it, if that's your real question. He can't possibly trace you here."

It was what she wanted to know, of course, but she still felt stung by his suspicions. He was the one who was in the wrong, and she resented his attempt to make her seem devious.

Watching him fell a tree did turn out to be exciting. Notching one side of the trunk, then swinging the heavy ax on the opposite side, he made the job look easy. His whole body was behind each powerful blow, sending chips flying and filling the air with resounding whacks. When the tree, not a giant compared to its neighbors but impressively large nevertheless, toppled to the ground, Gina found her heart was in her throat. There was unexpected drama in seeing the great weight of the tree crash to the ground, sending out vibrations that she could feel many yards away.

Leaning on the long ax handle, Jon pulled off his T-shirt, soaked from his exertions in spite of the coolness of the day, and wiped his face. Gina averted her eyes, wondering if she'd made a mistake in coming with him. His uncanny resemblance to Bruce made her terribly uncomfortable. It was too easy to imagine herself locked in his powerful arms, protected by his strength. How could he look so much like the man she adored, yet be so totally different?

"I need to go back for the power saw," he said, disappearing the way they'd come.

Left alone for a few minutes, she wandered among the trees, feeling insignificant compared to their towering heights. With no paths and few discernible landmarks, she became confused only a short way from the fallen tree and wouldn't have known which way to return if she hadn't heard the buzz of Jon's power saw.

"How do you like my woods?" he asked, pausing from his work when she came into view.

"Lovely," she said honestly enough, concealing the fact that she'd lost all sense of direction.

"Just remember it's easy to get lost if you're not familiar with the area."

"Of course, you don't have any ulterior motives for warning me," she said bitterly.

"I'm pretty sure you'd leave a trail I could follow," he said, "but be easy on yourself. Don't try leaving on your own."

"I've heard your warnings, all of them, but if you'd only listen to reason, you'd drive me back to Las Vegas yourself. This is my life you're playing with, Jon."

She was pleading, and she didn't care. Somehow she had to make him realize what he was doing to her.

"There isn't time for me to get my freedom and marry Bruce before he sails," she went on, encouraged because Jon had stopped working and was regarding her with a calm, level stare. "If you'll let me see Bruce and talk to him about what's happened, I'll agree to a long engagement. I can see that we should have taken more time to get to know each other, but you must have been in love yourself at least once. You must know how it feels when one person is the most important part of your life."

A change came over his face, and the glimmer of sympathy she'd detected for a brief moment faded.

"You're not going to die of a broken heart," he said, turning his back to her and effectively shutting out her pleas with the noise of the saw.

Late in the evening, with her arms and shoulders aching from volunteering to help take the wood back to the cabin area, she wandered outside. The darkness didn't seem threatening, in spite of Jon's warning to stay close to the building, and she desperately needed time alone to sort out her feelings and her options. She'd watched Jon unlock the van using a key he took from his pocket, but there was no way she could be sure he still had the ignition key in his possession. If she could stay awake longer than he did, she might get a chance to check the pockets in the clothing he wore that day. As tired as her body was, she didn't expect to fall asleep very quickly. Each passing hour spent as Jon's prisoner made her more uneasy; she was sure no risk was too great if she could get away from him and reach Bruce.

"Ready for bed?" he called out to her from the cabin doorway, his silhouette nearly filling the dimly lit opening.

"Not quite," she answered. "I'll come in a few minutes."

If she did find his keys, how could she get past him? With his mattress wedged in place against the door, she couldn't possibly open it. One thought did occur to her—the plastic covering made the mattress easy to slide on the bare floor. Was she strong enough to pull Jon and the mattress away from the door? Working very slowly and carefully, just inching it away enough to allow her to slip out, she might have a chance. With the van key in her possession, she only needed a few minutes' head start to get away. For the first time she felt a real surge of hope, and she had to compose her face carefully so he wouldn't suspect.

The night became a silent contest with Gina lying wide-eyed and anxious, straining to hear the even breathing that meant Jon was asleep. Instead of falling asleep immediately as he had before, he tossed restlessly, apparently as wide awake as she was. Once he got up and went outside, and she was terribly tempted to search his clothing while he was gone. Fortunately she didn't; he returned in a very short time, his attempt to be quiet not wholly successful.

Continuing her vigil, she monitored his every move until she felt her eyelids drooping and her determination to outlast him waning.

When she awoke, the cabin interior was murky, not fully dark as it had been. She lay motionless, trying to hear Jon, sure she'd missed her chance. He was breathing deeply and evenly, still sound asleep, and with luck he might remain asleep for a long time.

There wasn't enough light to see more than gray outlines, but she groped her way over to the wall where Jon had hung his jeans and woolen shirt. There were several pairs of jeans, the worn denim smooth to her touch, but it was too dark to distinguish one pair from the others. In the last pair she checked, the keys, secure in a small leather case, were in a side pocket.

Her hand was damp against the supple leather, and she glanced anxiously at the sleeping figure beside the door. Did people sleep more soundly at dawn or was the opposite true? Either way, she had little time to make good her escape. Neither speculating on her chances nor worrying about failure would help. Concentrating on being very quiet, she located her shoes and clothing, which she'd left in a neat pile with her purse the night before.

She wouldn't worry about dressing until she was in the van and well away from the cabin. Placing her makeshift bundle as close to the door as possible, she took the key case firmly between her teeth. There was no way she would risk misplacing it in the dark, and she needed both hands to pull the mattress with its slumbering occupant away from the entrance.

Praying that he wouldn't wake up, she gripped a bottom edge and was greatly relieved that she could move it. It was a slow, cumbersome job, but she managed to shift the mattress nearly a foot in easy stages, pausing often to make sure she hadn't disturbed Jon's sleep. So far her luck was holding.

With her bundle of clothing tucked in her arm and the key case in hand, she eased the door open, relieved that there was just enough room for her to squeeze through the opening. With freedom just steps away, she looked back at the dark shape of the man who no longer blocked her way.

"You're not going anywhere!"

His hand hooked around her ankle, throwing her off balance and making her drop her clothes.

"Let me go!"

"Not a chance! What do you think you're doing?"

He jumped up beside her, gripping her shoulders in his hard hands.

"You're hurting me."

The key case was still in her hand, but she had to find a way to hide it. Enough light was filtering into the room now to reveal every move she made as he towered angrily over her, his face hard and threatening.

"Do I need to ask where you were going?"

"Just outside. I couldn't sleep."

"You were going outside in your nightgown with a bundle of clothes and your purse?"

"I have a right to go wherever I like!"

"Not while you're my wife, you don't."

"Your wife by trickery and nothing else!"

He released her and slammed the door, reaching for his robe hanging on a near hook and giving her a moment to get rid of the key case. For lack of any alternative, she let it drop between the mattress and the door, hoping against hope that she'd have a chance to retrieve it before he found it.

"If you want to go outside, wake me," he said irritably, "but I think you had more than that in mind. Were you going to try walking down the mountain?"

"No! I just hate being held prisoner."

"You're not a prisoner. If you'd just try to be reasonable, Gina, you'd make things so much easier on yourself."

"Being here is the worst thing that ever happened to me. You just want me to be a docile prisoner so your job as jailer is easier."

"Believe me or not, but I don't like this situation either. I'm just not willing to let my brother squander the rest of his land on foolish marriages."

"What makes you an expert on marriage? How many wives have you had?"

"None," he said angrily.

"None but me!"

"This is a temporary arrangement, a legal convenience."

"Not temporary enough. I want to leave, Jon."

"You've said that, again and again. You'll leave when I'm ready to let you. Not until."

He looked scornfully at her clothing, purse, and shoes scattered on the floor where she'd dropped them, and she knew she had to find the key case and hide it immediately or lose her chance. Dropping to her knees, she slowly started gathering her belongings, edging closer to the spot where she'd dropped the key case. Hearing him walk softly across the cabin on bare feet, she thought it was safe to palm it.

She was wrong.

"My keys, please, Gina."

He was holding his jeans, looking so grim she knew she'd lost all chance of leaving in his van.

"Find them yourself," she cried out in angry disappointment, forcing the door against the mattress and pressing through the small opening.

"Gina!"

Her nightgown billowed in the breeze, providing scant protection from the chill of the morning. She ran without destination, blinded by tears of rage and frustration, pun-

80

ishing her bare feet on dry, sharp pine needles. Not until Jon caught her and pulled her into his arms did she realize he'd followed her.

All her fight was gone; she didn't protest when he scooped her up against his chest and carried her into the cabin, lowering her gently onto the bunk. Uncontrollable sobs shook her whole body as bitter tears flooded her face. All the misery she'd been storing away to face later was released in a torrent, and she barely noticed that he hadn't left her side. When he guided her head to a comfortable spot on his shoulder, she didn't have the will to resist.

Cried out at last, she became aware of his hand on her hair, stroking it as he whispered soft, meaningless words. Her escape attempt had been an utter failure, and she didn't even have enough pride left to push away this despicable man with Bruce's face.

"Things will work out, you'll see," he was saying.

"It's all wrong," she said brokenly.

Leaving her for a moment but immediately returning, he dabbed at her tear-streaked face with a tissue.

"Please, no more tears," he pleaded softly, cupping her flushed face in his hands.

The tears still in her eyes made her vision swim, and one drop trickled down from the corner of her lid. He was so near she could feel his breath, and dark bristles shadowed his still unshaven face. Stiffly, as though he were acting against his better judgment, he pressed his lips against her cheek, arresting the errant tear.

Closing her eyes, she squeezed out the last of the salty drops, and he kissed them away, too, tenderly but without hesitation, his touch cool on her burning cheeks. When her lips parted slightly, he traced their outline with one unsteady finger, then covered them with his mouth. His kiss was deep and warm, giving and satisfying, and his beard, where it touched her, was prickly, a new sensation that mingled pain and pleasure.

81

His robe parted to the waist as he leaned over her, and she pressed her cheek against the exposed flesh, hating her weakness but longing for his comfort.

His hands trailed over her bare shoulders, then pushed aside the slender straps of her nightgown. Swelling to fill his outspread fingers, her breasts felt electrified by his caress.

With a harsh sound that could have been an oath, he took her roughly into his arms, crushing her against his chest and kissing her with an abandon that shocked her to the core. Her mind shrieked in protest, but her senses reveled in his nearness. Torn between a burning need to accept him and an equally intense need to reject him, she was helpless. The decision was taken from her when he abruptly pulled away.

"I'm sorry." His voice was so strangled she could barely distinguish his words. "That was way out of line. It won't happen again."

"It . . . it wasn't all your fault," she managed to say, embarrassed by her own heated reaction.

He left the cabin, and she hastily washed and dressed for the day, as though her clothing were armor against the feelings that had taken them both by surprise.

When he returned a long time later, he looked damp and almost blue with cold, and she left the cabin quickly without a word. He found her some time later sitting beside the stream, lulled into a trance by the rapid flow of water over the clear, rocky bed.

"Come into the cabin," he said. "There's something I have to show you."

Mistaking her hesitation for fear of him, he backed up several steps.

"It won't happen again, Gina. I was out of line, and I sincerely apologize."

"I don't want apologies. I want to leave."

"Please, come inside."

82

She followed several steps behind him, wary of even accidental contact. When he sat down at the table, she did the same, keeping her chair far from his, making sure their knees wouldn't brush.

"This is the annulment agreement," he said solemnly. "I want you to read it and ask any questions you may have. Take plenty of time and be sure you understand every word of it."

"I don't need to read it. I'll sign anything to get my freedom."

"Read it," he insisted.

The *wherefores* and *parties of the first part* didn't sink into her mind, but she went through the motions of reading the legal document, turning the pages at the appropriate times even though she wasn't absorbing a word of it in her misery.

When she finally pushed it across the table to him, he shook his head dubiously.

"Tell me what it said."

"It's just a legal document. What difference does it make?"

"I don't think you read a word of it, Gina. Your mind was miles away."

Over her protests he read it line-by-line, explaining each section so carefully that she finally protested.

"I'm not stupid! I can read. I just don't care what it says."

"This last part may interest you."

He continued reading, ". . . to receive the sum of . . ."

The amount he read penetrated the wall she was trying to build, and she made him stop.

"Does that say you're going to give me all that money for an annulment?"

"In the payments specified, yes, provided this remains a confidential matter. I think the wording will hold up in

83

court, should you ever decide not to honor it. Let me finish."

"No, don't finish. I've heard enough. Whatever you may think, I'm not for sale, Jonathan Bradford Kenyon. I want this annulment for me, so I can marry Bruce, but I'll never sign that agreement the way you have it."

"Gina, be reasonable. It's a fair settlement."

"I don't want a settlement!"

"Don't count on Bruce marrying you. He has a habit of changing his mind, and he's not going to like your being married to me, however briefly."

"He will marry me. He loves me."

"The only way I'll permit him to marry is with a premarital contract that protects our family's property. If he hadn't been so impatient to marry you before his cruise, I would have convinced him of the importance of having one."

"I don't care about contracts or settlements or any of the things you're so hung up on. When I marry, really marry, it will be for love and nothing else."

"You won't leave this mountain until the agreement is signed, if it takes all winter. Accept the settlement, Gina. You won't be sorry."

"I'll sign it this instant, if you take out the part about buying me off."

"What are you saying?"

"I'll never take money from you. Never! Cross out the money part, and I'll sign it right now. Otherwise, you're going to spend the rest of your life keeping me prisoner."

"You're making a serious mistake, Gina. Do you realize what you're giving up? Security, a chance to do almost anything you'd like. You could travel, start your own business, live well for a while without working, if that's what you want."

"It isn't." Her voice was so low he had to strain to hear.

"I want to be free of you and your bribes and your insinuations and . . . everything."

"You're saying that if I remove the settlement agreement, you'll sign the rest?"

"Yes, exactly."

"I don't want it that way."

"You want me to take money so your conscience will be clear. If you can buy me off, it proves all the nasty things you thought before you ever met me. Well, you're not getting off that easily, Mr. Kenyon. I'll never sign an agreement that puts a price on my feelings. I wanted to marry Bruce because I love him. If you won't accept that, it's going to be a long winter!"

"You'll change your mind," he said wearily.

"No, I won't."

She watched woodenly as he gathered up the papers and locked them in the metal box.

"I'm going to start the van to charge the battery and check it out," he said. "Do you want to come with me?"

"No."

"I think I'd better lock the cabin then."

"You've changed your mind again about locking me in."

"After this morning, yes. Not because you can get away, but because you might hurt yourself trying."

"Can you convince yourself that's the reason?"

"I know it is."

She didn't follow his movements, but somehow she sensed that he was watching her from the cabin doorway.

"I am sorry for this morning," he said. "I can see why Bruce was so intent on marrying you."

When she looked up, the door was shut, and she could hear him securing the lock. She sat at the table a long time, completely oblivious to the fact that they'd forgotten breakfast.

After a long time she tried to pull herself together by

straightening up and cleaning the cabin. Jon didn't return; he was avoiding her, of course, but it was a relief to be alone. The prospect of spending days, weeks, maybe even months with him was unsettling, even frightening, and she didn't know how to cope with the things that were happening to her. Her only hope for a happy future was to reach Bruce, but how could she manage that?

Bruce. What was Bruce doing now? How was he taking her desertion? Would he believe that she'd deliberately stood him up? She was dreadfully afraid he would. But underneath her pain and disappointment, questions were nagging at her, prickly, difficult questions that she hadn't wanted to consider. Why didn't Bruce tell her more about his family? She could understand that he wanted to be loved for himself, not his wealth, but why had he been so secretive about other parts of his life?

For nearly a week they'd spent every possible moment together, talking endlessly about their lives, their hopes, their plans for the future. Why had Bruce omitted so many important things? Trying to find excuses for him, she could somewhat understand why he might regret his second marriage and want to conceal it, but why not tell her his brother was his twin? Would talking about his personal life open up parts of his past that he wanted to hide?

Pacing restlessly, she forced herself to think about the big question that had been plaguing her since she'd learned Jon's identity. What did she really know about Bruce? Was he the person his brother described, irresponsible, a womanizer, immature in his relationships? If he wasn't, if his brother was painting a black picture of his character for reasons of his own, it was even more urgent that she reach Bruce. She couldn't believe that she'd been totally wrong in seeing him as a loving, caring person. Where did the truth lie? Her head was pounding from the effort of trying to sort out facts and feelings, allegations and emotions.

A slight sound at the door made her freeze. Jon came in and stood behind her, and she couldn't bring herself to look at him. No matter what the truth about Bruce was, she had to face a very devastating truth about herself. When Jon had held her and kissed her, it didn't matter that he wasn't Bruce; she hadn't wanted him to stop.

Was she transferring her feelings for Bruce to his brother because of their physical resemblance? She didn't think so. Their personalities were entirely different, making the similarity in their appearances seem unimportant. It was easy to forget they were identical twins.

She had to get away from Jonathan! Just the fact that she had returned his kisses so eagerly was reason enough. He knew. He knew that she wouldn't have stopped him, and that gave him a terrible power over her, one she wanted to deny him at any cost.

"You must be hungry," he said.

It was an ordinary, mundane thing to say, but she couldn't bring herself to answer.

"I thought I'd do some sketching this afternoon. Will you come with me?"

His words sounded hollow, and his attempt at casual conversation fell flat.

"No, I'd rather not," she said.

"I'll stay here, then."

"No!" she said too quickly. "There's no reason for you to do that."

"Gina, there's no way we can avoid each other. We'll be spending quite a few more days in this cabin. Getting out during the day will make it easier."

"Take me back to Las Vegas."

"I can't."

"You won't."

"Either way, we stay here until Bruce's cruise begins and the annulment agreement is signed."

"I'll never agree to be bought off."

87

"I'm not buying you off. I'm trying to compensate you for a very unpleasant experience."

"No compensation can make up for ruining a person's life."

"Your life isn't ruined. There will be other opportunities, other men."

"You don't know that!"

"You're not a woman who will be alone for long."

Something in his tone made her turn and stare at him, but now it was his turn to avert his face. When he looked at her again, his face was an expressionless mask.

They went through the motions of eating like two actors rehearsing a new play, stiff, wary of each other, reluctant to help each other by volunteering any cues.

The whole day was formal, low-key, and painful, very painful. Gina avoided any mention of what had happened that morning, but it was there between them nevertheless. They took elaborate care not to have any personal contact, making a ritual of keeping distance between them, but it was futile. Both of them thought of little else, and each knew that the other couldn't forget it.

Finally in the afternoon they went for a long hike in the woods, both hoping to walk off some of the tension. He deliberately led her up steep embankments and over rough terrain, and she followed doggedly, glad to concentrate on physical obstacles, hoping, too, to discover some way back to civilization that he might be concealing. But if she expected or hoped to find a fire tower, a ranger station, or a passing hiker, she was disappointed. They were alone, totally isolated together on this remote mountain.

"Tired?" he asked after a particularly steep stretch of climbing.

It was obvious that she was out of breath and starting to drag behind, but she wouldn't admit it.

"No, only confused," she said, trying not to sound breathless. "Where are we?"

"We've circled above the waterfall. It's a little tricky getting down that way, but worth it for the view."

He was stretched out under a tree, unconsciously rubbing his left knee.

"Does your leg hurt?"

"No, hardly ever. It just stiffens up a little after a good workout."

"What happened to it?"

"Nothing that matters anymore. Let's get going. We should get past the waterfall before dark. It's too easy to have an accident if you can't see where you're going."

He hadn't exaggerated the beauty of the waterfall. Standing above it and watching the water cascade down was so impressive Gina felt weepy. It was a special, private place, a spot for lovers to share. The loveliness of it almost hurt.

Rejecting his offer of help, she scrambled down, hoping that the precarious footholds wouldn't break on her. He went first, checking behind him frequently to see if she was managing on her own. Fortunately, she was.

Their dinner was late and consisted of canned stew, carrot sticks, and biscuits. Gina didn't think she was hungry, but she ate ravenously. The strenuous exercise had exhausted her, and by unspoken agreement, they left the cleaning up until morning and went to bed early.

There was one change in the cabin that night. She draped the blanket to make a dressing room, but didn't take it down when she wrapped up in her sleeping bag for the night. Even though she didn't care much for the dark cubbyhole it created, the stuffiness seemed more bearable than knowing she'd see Jon on his mattress the moment she woke up.

When she did struggle back to full wakefulness in the morning, the blanket was gone, and Jon, fully dressed, was drinking coffee at the table.

"Why did you take the blanket?" she asked, unable to conceal her irritation.

"I thought it made the bunk too stuffy for you."

"At least let me decide that for myself!"

"Gina, a blanket isn't any defense if I want you."

She could only gasp and hope that he couldn't hear her wild heartbeats.

"Don't look that way. You're safe from me. I promised you that, and I won't go back on my word. What happened yesterday was an unfortunate mistake. It won't happen again."

His words were reassuring, but she lay facing the wall for a long time, wondering why she could still hear her heart pounding.

CHAPTER FIVE

Muffled sounds from the roof told her Jon was still working there, keeping busy with jobs that kept him as far from her as possible. She envied him the variety of things he found to do and wished her pride hadn't made her refuse his offer to use the sketch pad. Playing cards were spread in front of her on the bleached wood of the table, but the game of solitaire didn't hold her attention. Her hands kept busy shuffling through the deck and making an occasional play, but her mind was on other things. What if he fell off the roof and was seriously injured? Would he let her leave to bring help?

Knowing that her fantasies were running amuck again, she carelessly slapped a card on the table, bending a corner. Was there any reason compelling enough to force him to allow contact with the outside world? What if she convinced him there was illness in her family, a dying grandparent, perhaps? Would he let her make a phone call to her parents?

Flicking the corners of the deck impatiently, she knew the answer. It was too late to invent a plausible story, and Jon wasn't going to let her leave the mountain for any conceivable reason. She was serving time just as surely as if she'd been sentenced to jail. Anger rose like bile in her throat, and she pushed the cards together in a haphazard pile.

The door was standing open, and the air outside was unusually still, warmer than it had been since their arrival. An angry-sounding fly had invaded the room, its buzzing too insistent to be ignored.

"Don't you know your season is over?" she asked aloud, then had to smile at herself for talking to an insect.

There was a can of insecticide in the metal cabinet, but she decided the fly was welcome to the cabin if he wanted it. On impulse she picked up a corrugated cardboard carton that was now empty of supplies and serving as a waste receptacle. There were only a few paper wrappers in it now, so she stuffed them in the stove and went outside with the box.

As a small child she'd been an avid rock collector, pulling her treasures around in an old metal wagon her father had bought at a garage sale and repainted a bright orange for her. The only time she'd ever gotten into trouble with neighbors occurred when she'd quite innocently decided to add to her collection from a load of crushed stones newly spread around the shrubs next door.

The stream held a treasure trove of lovely, water-polished stones of all sizes and shapes that offered endless possibilities as doorstops, bookends, or just conversation pieces. The decorator in her decided to go rock hunting. She didn't even look up at Jon on the roof; from up there he could probably see where she went, but she wasn't going to make his role of jailer any easier by announcing her intentions.

The most appealing stones were those embedded in the bottom of the stream, but the water was too deep for wading without soaking her jeans. By working her way downstream she did find several along the shore line that were easily acquired, and one in particular was a real prize. Flat on the bottom and shaped like the cap of a giant mushroom, it was a mottled pink and gray worn smooth by centuries of water rushing over its surface. Gina was so pleased with it she decided to buff it with paste wax and use it as a bookend. Her find dried quickly in the sun while she searched for others, but none as pleasing caught her eye. She ended up with only four stones, but they made a heavy load, threatening to break through the bottom of the box.

"Gathering souvenirs?" Jon came up behind her so quietly that she started violently.

"The last thing I want is a souvenir of this."

She gestured with one hand, clutching the heavy box against her midriff. He took one side of the box, silently offering to carry it, but she held on. Strained to the limit, the bottom of the box collapsed and all four boulders thumped to the ground, sending them both scrambling backward to save their toes from being crushed. Jon fared the worst, landing on his seat on the ground and looking so surprised Gina laughed.

"That's the first time since you've been here," he said solemnly.

"What?" She was torn between laughing more and offering her hand to pull him up. She didn't do either.

"That you've laughed. You light up when you do. You should do it more often."

He was on his feet, looking at her intently, and she suddenly realized there was one great difference between the twins' appearances. Bruce's eyes were opaque, a warm brown but not highly polished, glinting with hidden lights as Jon's were. It was like the difference between an unpolished and a polished stone. If Bruce's were softer, Jon's were more compelling. Embarrassed by her observation, she looked away quickly and bent to retrieve her favorite stone.

"Let me help," he offered.

"No, I can get them."

"If you're going to carry away pieces of my real estate, at least let me make sure none of it lands on my feet."

"It was your fault the box broke."

"You wouldn't let go."

They were both stooping now, picking up the stones with their faces inches apart, but only her eyes were focused on the ground. She felt, rather than saw, his gaze locked on her, and confusion made her fumble with the pink and gray stone.

"I'll carry that," he said.

His fingers barely brushed hers, but it felt like an electric current had passed from his hand to hers. She backed away and stood upright, not caring about anything but getting away from him.

She walked away briskly, but he followed more slowly, carrying the four stones and the ruined box. When he placed them on the table, her mouth formed a word of thanks, but her heart begged him not to do this to her. Living with him, having him so close when his every gesture was a reminder of Bruce, was unbearable.

Awake in her bunk that night, uncomfortably warm behind the blanket she again insisted on hanging, she knew she had to get away regardless of how hard or risky it would be. None of her ideas so far had been very good, and this one probably wasn't either, but she was leaving in the morning. Jon took at least fifteen minutes bathing in the stream every morning. In that time she could be dressed and gone. Maybe he had exaggerated the distance to the nearest place, but even if he hadn't, she absolutely could not stay there with him any longer.

He would follow, of course, but knowing she had a head start, he'd probably use the van. She would parallel the road but stay concealed among the trees where he couldn't spot her. It wasn't a good plan, but it was all she had. She'd have to gamble that it would work.

After she was sure Jon was asleep, she rose and dressed in the dark, gathering together a few things to take with her. Some cans of food were all she wanted to carry, and fortunately she found an opener on a cabinet shelf. A pillow case served as her bag, and she fumbled around for a few more items picked almost at random, since she could hardly see what she was doing. Her purse and the nylon jacket Jon had loaned her were the last things she stuffed into the pillow case before she pushed it way down to the end of her sleeping bag to conceal it. When Jon went for his dip, she'd roll them up together and be gone. It was tempting not to bother with the bulky sleeping bag, but if she really did have to camp overnight, a warm covering could be a life-saver.

She slept surprisingly well, waking up when it was still dark. The soft, rustling noises of the night and Jon's breathing were the only sounds. It was tempting to try getting past him again, but two failures had convinced her he really was an incredibly light sleeper.

The full pillowcase at the bottom of her sleeping bag made her feet cramped, and she tried to stretch without creaking the infernally noisy bunk. For a moment she thought her restlessness had disturbed Jon, but he only shifted his position and went on sleeping. The temptation to go back to sleep herself was great, but she knew what an early riser he was. He might take his dip and return before she woke again, so she forced herself to stay alert.

It was eerie watching dawn invade the room, and much to her annoyance, an insistent buzzing told her the fly she'd spared yesterday was paying back her hospitality very ungraciously. At least the distraction helped her stay awake, and when Jon showed the first indications that he was ready to get up, she feigned sleep.

Alert to his every movement, she was maddened by the

pokiness of his morning routine. Why did he need to start the stove? It wasn't that cold! Didn't he know he might wake her if he banged around making coffee? Wouldn't that man ever leave to take his polar bear bath in the stream? She nearly panicked, worrying that he'd skip it just when her plans depended on the time he'd be gone.

At last he left the cabin, belatedly trying to be quiet by easing the door shut, but not locking it. She was up in an instant, but she had to confirm that he was heading toward the stream. His robe was gone, but she had to be certain. Pulling a chair to the window at the risk of looking ridiculous if he returned unexpectedly, she was just in time to see him walking toward the stream carrying his towel.

Every second counted. She rolled up the sleeping bag, thankful that it had strings to tie it into a bundle. The results were untidy, but she could worry about neatness later. The cold air hit her face outside the door, making her wish she'd kept the jacket handy, but time was more important than comfort.

The van sat in the clearing like a sluggish sentinel, and she was tempted to try letting air out of the tires just for spite. A moment's pause made her think more rationally, however. She was better off if Jon wasted time trying to find her with the van. If he started following her on foot, he would be much more alert to telltale sounds and visual clues. She didn't for a moment doubt that he saw things in the woods that she didn't, and that probably made him a good tracker.

Taking the woods to the left was an easy choice; on the right of the road there was a steep drop-off about fifty yards ahead. Once she'd put a comfortable distance between her and the cabin, she might risk crossing the road to make tracking her more difficult. Until then, she'd follow the easiest course. Her watch showed that Jon had been gone from the cabin nearly seven minutes. With her edge diminishing, she began running, wishing there were backstraps on her bedroll so she didn't have to carry it awkwardly in her arms.

Because the first part of the trip was downhill, she'd expected it to be easy, but each step was jarring her legs, and more tiring than she'd anticipated. Shifting her burden frequently, she kept careful track of the time. Ten minutes passed, then fifteen, and she knew Jon must be returning to the cabin. Nervously she moved deeper into the woods, noting where the early morning sun was rising so she could find her way back to the roadway. If she once lost her bearings, she'd never find her way out of the woods. Except for the sound of her own steps and her quickening breath, the woods were silent. She was still close enough to the road to hear the van when it passed, as she was sure it would, but hopefully no part of her was visible through the thick barrier of trees.

Eventually she had to slow her pace, and she was becoming increasingly uneasy because the stillness remained unbroken. Was Jon taking an especially long time for his dip? She couldn't be that lucky! Nor could she even hope that he wouldn't make good his threat to follow her.

When nearly an hour had passed and she was still alone in the woods, she should have felt elated. Instead, the lack of audible pursuit made her more nervous than ever. Her whole plan depended on Jon's wasting time following her in the van. If he was somewhere behind her on foot, he was almost certain to make up the difference in time before too long. He knew the woods well and moved so quickly with his long stride that she had as much chance as the little city rabbit had had with her dog.

She was perspiring from her haste, but the air was still cold. Thirst was becoming a problem, too; she hadn't expected to want a drink so soon after leaving. Veering deeper into the woods, she decided to chance unrolling the sleeping bag so she could take out the jacket to wear.

Her late night plundering hadn't been as successful as

she'd thought. True, she did have her purse and money, but they were useless until she reached some place to use them. Her blind selection of canned goods was near-disastrous. The large can she'd hoped was juice contained chow mein, and the smaller can was green beans. She might get hungry enough to eat them cold, but the packing liquid wouldn't do much for her thirst.

Doggedly she rerolled the bag, more comfortable now that she'd rested and put on the jacket, but still dry-mouthed and apprehensive. Worse, she was confused about directions. The sun seemed to her to have moved at a crazy angle, and she wasn't completely sure where the road was. Finding it became her first priority, but even knowing the general direction, she wasted a lot of time weaving her way back to within sight of the rutted car trail. Had she been too far away to hear the van pass? She didn't think so, but not being sure made her stomach knot and her palms dampen.

Rather than worry about getting lost, she decided to stay closer to the road. So far there was no sign of Jon in any direction, but the carpet of pine needles muffled sound. He could be only yards behind her on foot, and she wouldn't know it until he revealed himself. This thought was so unsettling she almost forgot to worry about bears and snakes, until she remembered reading once that rattlesnakes didn't necessarily rattle before they struck.

Traveling at a hard pace, she did pause once, catching just a glimpse of a white-tailed deer on the crest of a slope. A gray squirrel was her only real companion, perhaps forgetting fear in its anxiety to prepare for winter. Once, far above the treetops, she saw a bird soar with great outstretched wings, but she wasn't knowledgeable enough to be sure it was an eagle. She did know it could easily swoop down on any prey it chose, and she wondered if Jon would do the same to her. She was distrustful of the luck that had brought her this far, but a small hope was beginning to blossom. Maybe Jon would let her go. Maybe he wouldn't pursue her. She should be feeling happier than she was.

A slight sound startled her, and she remembered once reading a story in which a mountain cat had stalked a man for days. She'd been in junior high and really caught up in reading adventure stories; now she wished she'd never heard of mountain lions. Standing so still she stopped breathing to listen, she decided her imagination was playing tricks. Just for reassurance she made her way to the edge of the road again and peeked out. As long as the dirt roadway was on her right, she was sure to come to other people eventually.

Another hour passed, and she felt noticeably thirstier with each step and was beginning to feel hungry. Only the unappealing contents of her bundle made her keep walking instead of stopping for an early lunch break.

The next time the sound was louder, and she looked around frantically for a dead branch or stick to use as protection. Unfortunately, there was no such thing handy, and the first low, stick-like branch she tugged on was much too green to break away. Her heart was in her throat when she heard a louder and more definite noise.

Running now and trying to watch behind her for the source of the sound, she plunged forward, tripping on an unseen obstacle. The ground cushioned her fall enough to avoid injuries, but she was terribly frightened, realizing fully just how vulnerable she was alone in the woods.

"Gina!"

Relief and defeat mingled when she heard her name. Her heart was thumping and the bitter taste of failure filled her throat.

"How long have you known where I was?"

"A couple of hours, I guess."

99

"And you just followed me!"

"Yes."

"Why?"

"You seemed hell-bent on running around in the woods."

"You played with me, letting me think I could get away!" She was so angry her words came out in a staccato-like burst.

"I had to."

"To punish me!"

"To give my temper time to simmer down." He moved so close that all she could see was the plaid expanse of his shirt front. "If I had caught up with you two hours ago, you wouldn't be able to sit for a week."

"Are you going to add wife-beating to your other crimes?"

"Please, don't tempt me."

With cool deliberation, he pulled a canvas pack off his back and took out a canteen, holding it near her lips without relinquishing it. She reached for it, but he didn't give it to her, instead placing it near her mouth.

"I'll hold it. I don't intend to hike back without any water if you decide to throw it at me."

In spite of his distrustfulness, she was too dry to refuse. He let her drink deeply before taking a brief sip himself.

"What did you bring for lunch?" he asked with a slight grin she found maddening.

"Nothing."

Ignoring her he unrolled her sleeping bag and found the Chinese food and green beans.

"Well, if you prefer your menu to mine, you're welcome to it."

With easy experienced movements he spread a ground covering and laid out tinned meat, fruit, and biscuits left from the previous night, plus a bright yellow slab of cheddar cheese. To her utter amazement, he also had a bottle of white wine in his pack.

"You packed all that just to follow me?"

She was aghast at the appeal of the casual picnic spread out on the ground.

"I knew I'd find you."

Turning her back she moved away a few steps, too overcome to endure the game he seemed to be playing.

"Gina, come here."

His voice held a tender threat, and she obeyed unwillingly, afraid to force the confrontation that was simmering just below the surface.

She ate what he handed her and drank wine from a collapsible cup, not realizing how famished she'd been until she finished the hearty lunch. The wine relaxed her, and before the meal was finished, she lost track of how many times Jon refilled her cup. By the time he divided the last few drops between them, her head was swimming.

"If you're half as worn out as I think you are, you'd better rest a little while before we start back," he said, his voice seeming to come from a remote distance.

He spread out her sleeping bag, and she needed little urging to crawl into it. The last thing she remembered was seeing him lie back on the ground cover.

"Gina, wake up."

Groggy, with just a touch of a headache, she wiggled in her sleeping bag, trying to fit the contours of the ground more comfortably to her own curves.

"No, don't go back to sleep," he insisted. "We have to leave now to get back before dark."

"Did you sleep?" she asked, forgetting for the moment how angry she was at him.

"No, I didn't sleep," he said with a strange note in his voice.

"What time is it?"

"Time to go back," he said impatiently.

She didn't quite understand why he suddenly sounded so annoyed; she was the one who was humiliated and miserable, being taken back to a place where she didn't belong.

He was rolling up her bag and packing her loose items in his sack as though they went on wild chases through the woods every day.

"Jon, you have to let me leave here," she said desperately.

He stood then, his face hard and more than a little frightening.

"Don't you think I'd like to?"

His voice was so low and strangled that she automatically moved closer to hear him.

"I will not let you go back to Bruce."

Every word he said came out like the crack of a whip, and he moved so near to her that she felt the world closing in on her.

"I can't stay in the cabin with you," she whispered, knowing how true her words were.

She hadn't been running to Bruce; she'd been running away from Jonathan. Being so close to him night and day, seeing Bruce in his face but knowing in the secret recesses of her heart that Jon was more a man than his brother would ever be, she couldn't bear to stay. Didn't he see that she was being torn apart, loving Bruce but losing more of him every day as his more commanding brother stole into her heart little by little?

"You're coming back," he said, overwhelming her with his closeness.

She put out her hands, not knowing whether she was going to push him away or caress him, but the decision was taken from her. She was in his arms, trapped against the hard contours of his body.

He whispered her name in her hair, then tilted her face

to his, covering her mouth with a force that left her gasping for breath. His beard, grown long enough to begin softening, sent ripples of stunned delight through her face as he wedged an opening between the pearly edges of her teeth.

Pulling her gently to the ground covering, he covered her face with fierce little kisses, sending ripples from her temples to the sensitive lobes of her ear. Trailing downward to the hollow of her throat, his lips did miraculous things as an enticing warmth swelled within her.

Crushing her to the ground with his weight, he seemed caught up in the same spell that was shredding her will to confetti. With that special gentleness that only strong men have, he freed her breasts and lightly teased each nipple with his lips. Stroking and caressing, he built a fire that blinded her to time, place, and reason, and when he cast aside his shirt, she explored the hard ridges of his chest with trembling hands, thrown into a whirlpool of new sensations. For a brief moment they hung suspended, groping for a peak from which there was no return. Motionless, their hands sealed on each other's flesh, they paused, drinking in the full implication of what they were doing.

Like a man pulling himself out of a tar pit, he slowly rose until he stood over her with a look of consummate misery on his face.

"Not this way," he said hoarsely, turning from her with leaden movements.

She wanted to tell him it was all right, but the words caught in her throat and turned to sodden lumps choking off her words. Burning with her own needs, she felt nothing but compassion for those that ravaged him. With awkward fingers she struggled to replace her clothing, not for herself but because she sensed it would help him.

"I don't usually break my word so easily," he said,

keeping his back to her as he buttoned his shirt.

"Don't you see, Jon? I can't go back to the cabin with you."

"You're safe with me. If this doesn't prove it, nothing will."

"Why put yourself through this?"

"You're not going to run to Bruce," he said furiously, gathering up the ground cloth and finishing his preparations to leave.

"Why should that be your choice?" she pleaded.

"I started this. I'll finish it."

"You're making decisions for three people. You have no right to do that."

There was nothing new to add to her arguments, but she needed to say it all again, needed to convince herself that she was a victim, not a willing participant.

"Jon, please let me leave. For both our sakes."

"I won't even consider it."

He added her sleeping bag and other gear to his pack, only handing her the shoulder strap purse to carry.

"Let's go. We have a long walk."

His fast pace made her struggle to keep up, even after his leg seemed to stiffen, but she refused to ask him to go slower. When she fell behind, he glanced at her over his shoulder, but didn't stop to wait. They were nowhere near the road, as far as she could tell, and the woods seemed thicker than they had on her descent.

He finally did pause long enough for her to catch up, handing her the canteen to quench her thirst.

"I don't remember coming this way."

"It's rougher walking, but shorter," he said matter-of-factly.

"Can we rest a minute?"

"If you like."

He sat down first, stretching out his legs and massaging

104

his knee. Gina wanted to do it for him, but, of course, she didn't dare offer.

"Jon, we still have nearly two weeks before Bruce's cruise begins. How can we live together that long?"

"Drop it, Gina," he said angrily, pulling himself up and walking away, leaving her to hurry after him.

Oh, Jon, she cried out in her thoughts, *don't you see that I can't stay with you because I care too much?*

It was the truth, but she had trouble accepting it. Only days ago she'd been so sure Bruce was the only man she'd ever love. Now his domineering twin filled her mind and her heart so fully that she was frightened. Could she turn off her love for Bruce so easily? If she could, what was this feeling she had for Jon?

She loved him.

Improbable, irrational, inconsistent as her feelings were, they all centered on Jonathan. Was it physical attraction only, based on his uncanny resemblance to Bruce? Was she a shallow person, willing to give her heart away because a man was sensually exciting?

Jon was testing all her self-conceived notions. Agreeing to marry Bruce had been the single wildly impulsive act of her life, but shifting her love to his twin made her reel with confusion. She was a person who planned; her life was carefully structured. She knew her strengths and weaknesses, her talents and goals. Now nothing made any sense.

Underneath all her agitation, one awful possibility suggested itself. Jon would never let himself return her feelings, because Bruce had found her first. There was more between the brothers than she understood, of that she was sure. But was it honor that had made Jon stop their lovemaking? Or had he rejected her because, in his eyes, she was Bruce's woman?

Half-running to keep up with him, she welcomed the exhausting pace; it made her too tired to think, to dwell on a whole new set of disturbing thoughts. All she knew for sure was that if Jon turned to her, she would open her arms to welcome him.

Lost in thought, she never saw the treacherous branch until it caught her full in the face, knocking her backward but not before it raked across one cheek. Her soft outcry brought Jon running back to her side.

"Are you all right?"

"I didn't see it," she said, automatically putting her hand to a raw-feeling spot on her face. Her fingers came away wet with blood.

"You've cut your cheek," he said, concern clouding his face. "Let me see."

Cupping her chin in one hand, he studied the damage with hooded eyes, taking out a handkerchief to blot the trickle of blood.

"A nasty scratch, but I don't think it's deep. I will have to clean it right away," he said.

She endured his ministrations as he poured water from the canteen on a clean handkerchief and none-too-gently washed away the dirt.

"Sorry," he said when she winced. "I have to be sure it's clean."

The dull throbbing in her cheek was much easier to bear than Jon's nearness, his hands on her face, the concern in his expression.

"It's nothing," she said impatiently, finding pity a poor substitute for what she wanted from him.

"Just a minute. I have the small first-aid kit with me. I want to put on some medication and a gauze pad."

"And what you want, you do," she said sullenly, hiding her true feelings behind a mask of irritation.

"No."

His word hung there between them, heavy with a meaning that had nothing to do with first aid.

"We're going to have to talk," he said, avoiding her eyes by fumbling with the small plastic box that held the medical kit.

"There's nothing to say."

She recoiled when he doused her cheek with stinging antiseptic, then applied what looked like a giant-sized Band-Aid, a pad with tape attached.

"You're prepared for everything, aren't you?" she asked unhappily.

"No. I wasn't prepared for you."

Wanting him to say things directly, instead of making vague statements that could be interpreted several ways, she didn't answer.

"Gina, this situation between us isn't going to go away."

"Then the solution is to let me go."

"No, it isn't! Can't you realize yet that Bruce will bring you nothing but unhappiness?"

"You've taken away my right to learn that for myself."

"Only a fool has to learn the stove is hot by touching it."

"I'm not a fool. I won't be talked to as if I were!"

He replaced the kit in his pack, then looked into her eyes with a steely expression.

"Look at the facts, then." He reached out to smooth an edge of tape on her cheek, but she backed away. "I was only pressing the tape down."

"Thank you. You've done your Boy Scout good deed. I'll be fine."

"Sarcasm doesn't become you, Gina."

If he would only argue, raise his voice, become nasty, she could defend herself. The gentleness and concern in his voice were devastating, making her feel like a child being rebuked for willfulness. It wasn't fair! She turned her back and started walking.

He waited several moments, then called out, "That's not the way."

Turning to face him, she thought she caught a glint of amusement on his face. It was quickly veiled.

"Well, if you know which way to go, go," she said.

"In a minute. I want you to understand something before we go back to the cabin."

Defeat and exhaustion played over her features as he waited for her to come closer.

"I won't deny that I want you very much," he said hoarsely, "but I can't take advantage of this situation and keep my own self-respect. Do you know what I'm saying?"

She didn't. Was he too honorable to have a fling with her after making a hopeless muddle of her life, or was he too proud to take his brother's woman?

"It doesn't matter," she said woodenly.

"It does. We have a long haul ahead. I want you to know you're safe with me, that I'll live up to all of our agreement."

"We have no agreement," she said angrily. "This is your show, all of it. The only thing I'll agree to is an annulment without a settlement. None of this was my idea, and I won't play by your rules."

"You have no choice," he said sternly. "I only wish you'd let me make it easier for you."

Turning her face away, she froze out any further efforts on his part to discuss their situation. Feeling the way she did about him, admitting it to herself, everything he said only caused more pain. Couldn't he see that she cared about him, even loved him?

He couldn't, and she would never tell him.

The rest of the hike back to the cabin was an ordeal. Her cheek burned, and the rest of her face seemed to be criss-crossed with little scratches. Her legs ached from the unaccustomed climbing, and she was thirsty, cold, and weary. Still, all of her discomfort would have vanished in an instant if Jon had turned to take her in his arms.

Instead he raced ahead, pushing himself and leaving her to trail behind, in sight but too far back for conversation. It disturbed her that, when she finally saw it, the cabin looked like home.

CHAPTER SIX

A storm warning was in the air. They both awoke sensing it, and no media-produced weather forecast was necessary to confirm it.

"It feels like rain," Gina said, hugging the sleeping bag under her chin, not wanting to get up and face another day that promised nothing but frustration.

"More than that, I think. We may get a real storm. Turn around. I'm going to get dressed."

She felt a renewed flash of anger that he'd been so high-handed about not letting her drape the blanket beside her bunk, but she resented it mainly because he'd been right. The privacy wasn't worth the stuffy, closed-in feeling. Lazily she rolled over to face the wall, but not seeing Jon didn't make her any less conscious of every move he made. When he was in the cabin, the room seemed crowded.

"If you want to go outside, you'd better do it now. I don't like the feel of this storm that's coming."

"Where are you going?"

"To haul up food supplies before it starts raining."

"I'm running out of clothes," she stated.

"We'll do some laundry later. Maybe there'll be enough water in the cistern so we won't need to carry it from the stream."

It was an exaggeration that she was short on clothes; her packing had been planned to cover a long, carefree honeymoon. What she didn't have was clothing suited to cabin living. Her two pairs of jeans were unappealingly soiled, so she had little choice but to put on a pair of pale beige dress slacks in a crisp linen-like fabric, part of a good pantsuit. With a patterned blouse in neutral and cocoa shades, she looked better than she wanted to look.

She had plenty of time between Jon's trips to make up her face, but she didn't bother. Making herself attractive for a man who was treating her like a piece of furniture, as he had since their return last night, was the last thing she'd do, and the bandage hid part of her face anyway. It would be a relief when she could relax in clean jeans and a sloppy shirt again. Just to ruin the effect of her attractive outfit, she helped herself to one of Jon's remaining clean shirts, a cotton plaid flannel that clashed horribly with her blouse.

"That's a bizarre combination," he said dryly when he carried another load of food supplies into the cabin.

"I'm sorry if you object to my borrowing your shirt."

"Borrow whatever you like," he said, completely unruffled.

The stove overheated the cabin, forcing her to discard his shirt, but it did nothing to dispel the overcharged atmosphere in the cabin. The feeling that a storm was coming made them hurry through their chores. Gina helped Jon carry extra water to the cabin, filling all available kettles and basins, but the way the sky looked, a lack of water wasn't going to be their problem.

Helping him unpack food supplies, she was surprised at the variety. Besides dried foodstuffs like beans, rice, potatoes, milk, and eggs, the store included a pleasing

111

assortment of mixes, beverages, and even dehydrated dinners. For varying their menus even more they had gelatin mix, peanut butter, mixed nuts, dried fruit, chocolate bars, lemon drops, and even vitamin C. True, they would have to rely on tinned meats and salami if Jon couldn't fish, but she knew now that he had told the truth: they could winter in the cabin without any undue hardship in the food line.

"Why are you bringing all this up from the van now?" she asked, putting a box of oatmeal on the shelf.

"Two reasons. I don't think we'll be leaving the cabin in the next few days."

"And the other?"

"So you won't be tempted to take it for a foray into the woods."

Flushing deeply, she was reminded of how sore her cheek was. She hadn't had enough courage to peel off the pad and examine the damage in her makeup mirror. Touching the edges of the pad, she unintentionally called his attention to it.

"When we're done with this, I want to check that scratch of yours."

"I can take care of it myself."

"Probably, but I intend to see for myself that there's no infection."

Far from forgetting it when the food was put away, he insisted that she sit at the table and let him see her cut. The easiest thing was to let him get it over with, so she reluctantly sat while he removed the soiled bandage.

"It looks pretty good."

His fingers on her cheek were gentle, touching her only as much as was necessary to remove the pad, but his hand revived sensations she wanted to forget.

"You're not going to like me for it, but I've got to reclean it and put on some antibiotic ointment," he said.

"Is it infected?"

"No, not at all. Just a precaution."

He laid out the things he needed in orderly fashion on the table.

"I'm afraid this will sting," he said sympathetically.

Sting wasn't the word! It felt like a burning arrow was injected into her cheek. Pure reflex made her jerk away, so he pressed her head against his body so he could work quickly. She trembled and prayed he would attribute it to the pain, not the real cause, being in contact with him. Shutting her eyes to mask her thoughts didn't dull the sensations that were rocking her. How could he think they were able to live together like casual acquaintances?

"Hurt?" he asked with a worried tone.

"A little," she said, unwilling to admit that it hurt a whole lot.

"I'm sure it's not deep enough to leave a scar."

She hadn't been worried about that possibility and wished he hadn't mentioned it.

Did he hold her head against his torso just a moment longer than necessary? She was sure of it, but nothing in his nonchalant manner revealed whether touching her stirred him too.

"Leave the bandage on all day, and we'll see how it is tomorrow."

He moved away, making her feel very, very alone.

The thunder started first, booming across the mountain in the overcharged atmosphere like the opening burst of cannon fire in a great battle. The trees that made the retreat a shady haven on calm days seemed to sway in the wind like battering rams threatening to crush their tiny shelter if the god of war so commanded them.

Storms along Lake Michigan's western shore could be wet, nasty, even violent, but never had Gina felt so threatened by one. In the little cabin they were exposed to the full force that nature could muster against them, and she was scared enough to wish she wasn't too old to hide her head under a pillow.

113

From the doorway she could see jagged cracks of lightning splitting the sky, aimed at the thousands of towering pines that surrounded them. Once she heard a tremendous, resounding thud, then Jon was beside her, pulling her back from the door and shutting it.

"We need rain badly," he said matter-of-factly to cover his abrupt reaction.

"Did lightning hit a tree? What if it starts a fire?" she asked worriedly.

"It's a possibility, but I think we're in for a rain that will put out any kind of blaze before it gets a good start."

Except for the one inside the cabin, Gina thought dejectedly, realizing what the storm meant to the two of them. Until it stopped, they were stuck together in this single room, so confined that they would have to plan their ordinary movements so they wouldn't touch each other. How long could either of them endure such close contact?

At that moment she knew that the last thing she wanted was a loveless easing of their mutual passion, but nature itself seemed to be conspiring against her.

When the rain began, the wind blew it with such force that they had to shut the small windows. Jon let the stove burn down to glowing embers, suggesting they wear coats instead of heating the cabin to the point of suffocation. Without the nylon jacket Gina was cold, but wearing it she was too warm. Try as she might, she couldn't convince herself that her discomfort was caused by the storm, the temperature, or the almost nonexistent fumes of the stove.

"We might as well have breakfast. The water's hot enough for tea and oatmeal, if that's okay with you," he offered.

"Anything is fine."

She'd forgotten they hadn't eaten.

There was only so much routine work involved in a meal. All too soon they were finished with the last of the cleaning, the dishes washed and dried, the stove gleaming,

114

and the table scrubbed. The day stretched ahead endlessly. The rain bombarded the tin roof, making a racket that discouraged conversation in ordinary tones, and this effect of the storm suited them both.

Gina browsed through the cabin's selection of reading material and found a paperback that looked promising, a disaster book. At least it fit her mood. She sat at the table to read, needing to catch as much light as possible from the small windows.

"Would you mind if I sketched you?"

"What?" She'd heard, but felt uncomfortable with the idea.

"Draw you. You wouldn't need to do anything. Just keep reading as you are."

There was no reasonable excuse for objecting. He had to entertain himself some way. Still she was uneasy.

"I thought you drew wildlife."

"I draw anything that catches my attention. It's only a hobby."

"You're good, though. Do you do paintings from your sketches?"

"I rarely have time. Maybe someday. I never throw one away, hoping I'll have more time in the future. Coming here is usually my only vacation of the year. Would you mind changing chairs? The light would be better."

She moved, conscious of his intent stare. Determined to seem as unruffled as he was, she turned her attention back to the book. In the story a brilliant young scientist was bucking the establishment, trying to convince them of danger. She was alive to danger herself, both within and without the confines of the cabin. Concentrating on the book was impossible, but she kept turning pages so Jon wouldn't realize it.

"I like the way your hair falls over your cheek. It looks so soft."

She was startled until she realized he was talking as an artist, not a man.

Time seemed to drag. If she'd been able to concentrate on reading, she'd be halfway through the book. Her bottom was getting tired from sitting on the hard wooden chair, and she wanted to stretch every muscle in her body.

"I'm tired of sitting," she said at last.

"I'm sorry; I was so wrapped up in drawing, I didn't realize how long you've sat still. Thank you for being such a patient model."

"Did you finish?"

"Almost, but I'm not going to show it to you."

"That's not fair after I posed all this time."

She stood and flexed her almost numb seat.

"You won't like it," he assured her, closing the pad to conceal his drawing.

"I might, but I don't care much for modeling, that's for sure. It must be a hard way to make a living."

"What about your way? Do you like what you do?"

"Pretty much. I'd like to do more actual designing. My boss keeps me busy ordering wallpaper, working with the people who make our drapes, running to sales, that sort of thing. But it's interesting. I never stop learning."

"Want some tea?" he asked, moving to the stove to pour himself some leftover coffee.

Actually she didn't. Visiting the outhouse in the driving rain was something she'd like to postpone as long as possible, but a mischievous imp prompted her to give him something to do. Distracted by the routine of making her tea, he didn't notice when she quickly thumbed through his sketches, locating his latest one in a matter of seconds.

"How dare you!" she gasped.

He turned angrily, taking the pad away from her.

"I told you it wouldn't please you."

"I didn't know you were doing a centerfold!"

"That is the most childish remark you could make.

You've studied art. Where on earth did you get your prudish ideas about the human body?"

"My body! I sat there fully clothed, and you undressed me on your pad."

"I drew you engrossed in a book, sitting at a table, nude to the waist."

"Which I wasn't!"

"I didn't need to see your breasts again to remember how beautiful they are."

He tore a sheet from the pad, crumpling it in his hands and tossing it into the stove. One short-lived flame shot up, then the blackened ruins crumbled into ashes.

"It may have been the best thing I ever did," he said regretfully.

His smile was ironic, but she was too angry to back down.

"Never draw me again."

"If that's what you want."

He grabbed the only rain slicker in the cabin and went outside, even though she protested that there was still too much lightning. The storm drove him back in a short time, but the minutes alone were long, lonely ones for Gina. He was right about nude studies; every art student drew many, seeing the model as a subject, not a person. She'd overreacted because of her own feelings for him. Having him treat her body so casually hurt her pride more than it offended her, but his comment about her breasts made her uncomfortable in another way.

Rain streamed from his face and hair when he returned, and she tried to ignore him as he toweled himself dry and put his sodden boots near the stove to dry.

After a silent lunch, he suggested that they play gin rummy. She couldn't think of a reason for refusing.

"That's twelve dollars and eighteen cents you owe me," he said after a long game she'd lost by letting her attention wander. "Do you know any games you're good at?"

"None," she admitted.

They were walking on eggs with each other, avoiding so many subjects that it was easier not to talk. The rain eventually lessened, so she ventured outside, returning with the bottoms of her slacks soaked and her shoes plastered with mud.

"If this rain doesn't stop soon, the cabin is going to float down the mountain," she said.

"No, we're pretty secure here. What I worry about is the road. We may have some washouts if this keeps up."

"Then how will we leave here?"

"If the road is impassable, I'll have to walk out and get a bulldozer up here. If not, we wait for the mud to dry."

"I hope you're exaggerating."

"So do I."

By the next morning the rain had slowed to a depressing drizzle, but the soft ground surrounding the cabin made any excursion a messy trek. They washed a few clothes by boiling them on the stove and hanging them on a cord tied on hooks, cutting off one corner of the cabin. The garments steamed as they dried in the over-heated air, filling the room with the smell of wet laundry. Jockey shorts, socks and jeans drying inside made the cabin look squalid.

In the afternoon Jon did the only thing sensible on such a dreary day; he napped. Gina envied him, but she was too restless to sleep. She paced, puttered, and tried to read, remembering the countless little skirmishes they'd had that morning, meaningless little disagreements that built up because they were both irritable. He was doing them both a favor by sleeping, but Gina found it a torture to keep from looking at him, his hair framing features serene in rest, his limbs outstretched like a man spread-eagled on stakes, his stomach as flat as an athlete's.

A long sleep did nothing to improve his disposition. He awoke to find her scraping the mud from his boots onto a piece of paper on the table.

"You don't need to clean my boots."

"They're filthy, and there's nothing else to do."

"I'll do them myself."

Refusing to let him bully her, she went on, even after he came up to her. Annoyed that she ignored him, he slapped her lightly on the bottom. It barely smarted but, resenting it mightily, she sent his boots flying across the room and sought sanctuary in the far corner of her bunk.

Seconds later, their sense of the ridiculous surfaced, and they laughed simultaneously.

"I think it's called cabin fever," he said, smiling apologetically.

"There's a lot of that going around in here," she agreed.

Just for something to do, she went over and felt several of the still-damp clothes on the line.

"Still wet?"

She nodded.

"Something else that may be wet is my battery. I think I'll go start the van and dry it out."

The rain was only a drizzle now, and he left the slicker on its hook. On impulse she put it on herself and waited with the door open only a crack until he was out of sight. To start the van, he needed a key, a key he was concealing somewhere outside the cabin, she suspected.

She followed him at a distance, keeping a thick-trunked tree between them wherever possible. The motor was running by the time she had the van in her line of vision from a concealed vantage point. Once he jumped out and checked the motor, then got back inside, apparently not at all worried about running out of gas by idling it too long. Did that mean there was a station closer than he'd led her to believe? Her wild speculations were at least entertaining.

Poised for flight if necessary, she finally saw him relock the door, walk around to the back, and stoop beside it. That was it! She couldn't see exactly where he put the keys, but she was willing to bet he had them attached with a magnet to the underside of the van.

Running to get back to the cabin before he saw her, she waited for the elation to hit her. It never did. After trying so hard, she could safely and easily leave as soon as the roads dried. Why didn't the prospect make her happy?

She hung up the slicker, rubbing it with a towel so Jon wouldn't notice it was wet. A scarf had kept her hair dry, but she'd forgotten one thing: the drizzle had soaked her bandage, making it stick painfully to her cheek. Jon was sure to notice it and know she'd been outside.

Yanking blindly, she felt the tape, fortunately the painless kind, give way. The telltale bandage was smoking in the stove and she was examining the scratch in her cosmetic mirror when Jon returned.

"It looks all right," he reassured her, stripping off his damp jacket.

He bent over her, running one finger along her chin line. That was all, one finger barely caressing her, but it touched her deeply, making her want him more than was humanly possible. For an instant both their faces were naked, and the desire was there, a tangible, compelling force. The mirror fell from her hand, but he caught it, saving it from splintering on the hard floor.

"You have quick reflexes," she said, trying to sound casual.

"I wonder," he whispered, his lips descending in a way that could only shatter their mutual defenses.

"My face hurts," she blurted out desperately. "I was going to rebandage it."

"I'll do it," he said quickly, doing his part to break the spell.

The hurt wasn't in her cheek. Inside she was aching with a fierceness that made her hands tremble and her whole body tense. She closed her eyes tightly, imagining that she felt his hands stroking her breasts again, not

120

knowing how she could endure another moment without flinging herself into his arms.

Bruce had never made her feel like this. If she needed proof that her feelings for Jon had a depth she'd never before experienced, her body was giving it to her now.

What did she really know about the man who was solemnly bandaging her cheek? She knew he was strong and suspected that he was a good person but, like his brother, he concealed part of himself from her. Hanging back, not committing himself, was he using honor and self-respect as a shield against his own vulnerability?

Two men, two mistakes, she thought miserably. Practical, cautious Gina was caught on the two horns of a dilemma, loving first one brother, then the other, sure of her passion, unsure of her emotions.

At first when she'd looked at Jon, she saw Bruce. Now she looked at him and forgot Bruce. Had a substitute become the object of her love so easily? Was her love as shallow as his brother claimed Bruce's was?

All she knew was that at that moment, Jon completely filled her heart, her mind, her world. She wouldn't be able to deny him even her soul if he demanded it.

Standing slowly after he patted on the new bandage, she didn't dare look into his face. If she saw rejection there now, she would shatter into a million brittle bits.

Pulling her into his arms, he kissed her in a way completely outside all of her experience, making the flesh of her lips quiver with longing, filling her mouth, drawing out sweetness as fiery bolts of desire shot through her and his own need grew, swelling and insistent.

There could only be one conclusion. She worked her hands under his shirt, reveling in the warmth of his back and the smooth play of muscles under her touch.

"This shouldn't happen," he choked, but his arms belied his words as he pressed her even closer, hurting her with the force of his kiss.

121

Then he was gone. Stunned, cold, empty, Gina stared at the open door. The shock was like the death of a loved one. She had been so sure he'd stay with her, make love to her, fulfill her in every way a man can, that she couldn't believe he'd left her.

At first she worried because he was coatless, wandering outside soaked to the skin. Dusk would come early, and the rain had brought with it a chill that penetrated the cabin in spite of the stove's best efforts. Later, forgetting about dinner, she grew increasingly anxious. An hour passed and more, and he hadn't returned. At last, her imaginings drove her outside.

"Jon! Jon!"

Her voice sounded shrill in the stillness of the wilderness evening, but it didn't bring an answering response. There was only one place where Jon could take shelter, and that was the van.

Feeling lost and cold, but pushed on by her growing anxiety, she made her way down toward the van, watching her step but not carefully enough. The ground, slippery from the drenching rain, made poor footing, and she stumbled, sliding to a stop on her back, unhurt but soaked. The back of her slacks clung wetly to her legs and hips, cold and clammy against her skin.

Her trip had told her all there was to know. The van was gone. Her first reaction was disbelief that Jon had left her alone on this storm-ravaged mountain, but it was followed immediately by anger, raw burning fury that he had deserted her after keeping her a prisoner for days.

Tears of rage streamed down her face as she retraced her route, sliding back a step for every two she went forward. When she finally got back to the cabin, she wanted to throw things, tear the place apart, shatter everything inside the room. Instead she cried noisily, so angry with Jon she wanted to scream it to the mountainside.

Sometime near midnight she heated a can of beef noodle

soup, hoping food would ease the headache she always got when she cried. Traces of her anger still played at the edges of her consciousness, but something else was replacing it: worry. The roads were slippery and could have washed out in spots; the van had been outside in the deluge, possibly dampening the brakes. Certainly the tires would slide easily on the dirt surface, making any drive hazardous at best. Jon could so easily have an accident, stranded miles from help, perhaps hurt himself, bleeding, even dying, for lack of medical attention. She was the only person in the world who knew he was out there, and it might take her a day or more to reach him on foot. When she did, there was no way she could carry him away from a crushed van. Jon could die on that isolated mountain road, and there was nothing she could do quickly enough to help. Never again would she take an automobile or a telephone for granted!

Her heart was pounding inside her rib cage, and her first instinct was to set out immediately on foot.

The night outside was black; the pale light escaping from the cabin reflected on the puddles and ruts. Stepping a few feet from the building, she could barely see three feet ahead. Her chances of negotiating the mud-slicked mountain in the dark were so poor her heart sank. What good could she be to Jon if she lost her footing and seriously hurt herself? She would have to wait for daylight, even though every passing moment was a torment. If she had needed proof that she loved Jon, the agony of possibly losing him forever more than supplied it.

Her mood swung from anxiety to anger to outright fear. Just when she thought she'd go crazy with worry, another possibility occurred to her. She was underestimating Jon. He was fully capable of taking care of himself in any situation. Stripped of her frenzied imaginings, his departure demonstrated one thing. He was completely in control of the situation. He could come and go as he pleased;

she was the prisoner. At this moment he most likely was enjoying himself in some remote country bar, listening to music, talking with the local people, quenching his thirst, and completely forgetting her alone in the cabin.

Thinking of her own situation, she hurried to the door and slid the heavy bolt into place, praying that no enraged bear would try to raid the cabin that night.

How could he leave her, vulnerable and unprotected? This was his world, not hers. Remembering his rifle, she took it from its hiding place and opened the canvas case. The weapon was useless to her; even if she could fire it in a moment of desperation, she hadn't the slightest idea how to load it. Besides, the ammunition was locked away in the metal box and the key hung around his neck. She would never forgive that man for leaving her here alone, the victim of her own imagination, if nothing else.

Sometime near dawn she dozed off, exhausted by anger and her restless longing for a house with windows at eye level so she wouldn't feel so entombed.

A far-away pounding penetrated her dream, and she unwillingly surfaced, taking a few moments to realize that the noise came from outside the door. Remembering her solitude, she was more than a little afraid to open it for an unidentified knocker. Reassuring herself that it had to be Jon, she slid back the bolt and opened the door a crack.

"Let me in," Jon said crossly.

She threw back the door and darted across the room, whirling to face him with undisguised fury on her face.

"Did you have a nice night on the town?"

"I had a lousy night sleeping in the van, and I'm frozen to my bones."

"You don't need to bother lying to me."

"Gina, I have no reason to lie, and you sound like a nagging wife."

"I am a wife, but not by choice. The least you can do

after tricking me into coming here is not desert me and throw me to the bears."

"I don't see any bears."

"Oh, be cute! You're the one who tried to scare me silly about grizzlies."

"In five years I've yet to see a bear here."

"Then you lied to me."

"No, I warned you to take reasonable precautions and not go flying down the mountain at night."

"But that advice doesn't apply to you."

"You've let the stove go out," he said wearily.

"I forgot it. Next time you leave, maybe you can leave me a list of orders to follow while you're out playing."

"I've seen how you follow orders, and I don't know where you got the crazy idea that I've been having fun. Have you ever slept all night in a van with only one grease-stained blanket?"

He started working on the stove, feeding bits of kindling to a blazing wad of newspaper brought there for that purpose.

"I know the van was gone," she said with more hurt than anger now, sure that he had lied to her. "I went down to the clearing last night."

"All right, if you want a minute-by-minute account, I drove down a way to check the road. It's slick from rain but I didn't see any serious problems. As soon as I came to a turn-around point, I turned around."

"But you didn't come back to the cabin."

"No," he said keeping his back to her.

"You let me think you might be hurt, lying along the road with the van smashed to bits."

"Were you worried about me, Gina?"

He turned and smiled at her, a taunting grin that re-fueled her anger.

"I was worried about being stuck here alone with no

125

transportation," she lied vindictively, unable to bear the implication that he was important to her.

"So you wouldn't be able to get back to Bruce."

"Yes!"

"I don't care if you yell at me for being out all night," he said grimly, moving close and blocking her retreat, "but don't talk to me about Bruce."

"You brought him up! He's the issue, isn't he? You have no right to steal your brother's wife."

"You aren't my brother's wife. You're mine, and you'll stay mine until Bruce is gone and the agreement is signed, so you might start acting like a wife."

His closeness and his words made her misinterpret his intentions, and she groped for a way to defend herself.

"If you touch me, you'll regret it!"

"I have no intention of doing so. Make me some breakfast while I wash up."

Was it relief she felt that he only wanted breakfast? A confusing barrage of feelings made her stumble awkwardly toward the cabinet and stare at the food packages without removing any.

"Pancakes will be fine."

He reached around her and forced a package into her hands.

Carefully, reading directions, making unnecessary preparations and false starts, too conscious of his movements to concentrate, she finally managed to begin the meal. He stood only too near, vigorously scrubbing his torso and arms, dipping the washcloth into a basin of cold water.

"Why don't you wait until the water is hot?" she asked, keeping her eyes averted.

"Worry about breakfast."

A chance glance in his direction showed her that he was toweling his chest until it was red, seemingly intent on removing at least a layer of skin.

126

She burned a pan of pancakes, reducing them to charred slabs fit for nothing but the fire, but finally a presentable meal was on the table. At least he didn't comment on her mistake, even though the odor of burnt dough hung heavily in the air. He ate heartily, reminding her that, if his story was true, he'd missed dinner, but she only picked at one pancake. If he noticed her lack of appetite, he didn't comment on that either. In fact, the meal was consumed in total silence, a stiff, uncomfortable lack of conversation, not the companionable quietness of people who are happy with each other.

Afterward, she tried to count on her fingers the number of days until Bruce left on his cruise. She wished for a calendar and remembered a wallet-sized one in her purse. On second thought, she didn't look at it. From now on she would count hours, not days. She knew where Jon kept the keys to the van. All she needed was a dry day to drain the road and make it safe for her flight. Jonathan Bradford Kenyon wasn't going to keep her there against her will until Bruce's cruise began. Of that she was certain.

CHAPTER SEVEN

Instead of stopping, the rain furiously pelted the roof again that afternoon, making them virtual prisoners of the weather. Their laundry did dry, finally, and Gina took hers off the line and folded it, wanting to change from her skirt into jeans but not while Jon was in the cabin. When she was done, she mentioned that his clothing was dry too but it was hours later before he put it away. Doing it for him was just too cozily domestic.

He puttered without seeming to accomplish anything except to agitate her. Whenever she thought she was far enough away from his activity to avoid him, he invaded her space, making her realize how roomy her apartment was compared to the tiny cabin. She and Claire never got in each other's way, except for an occasional rush on the bath when both were going out at the same time. Of course, she'd never been so keenly aware of another person as she was of Jon. His restless energy, coupled with an economy of movement that showed his self-control, made him an impossible man to ignore. Whether she looked at him or not, she sensed his every motion, and he was driving her to distraction.

128

Unwisely, she began playing the "what if?" game. What if Jon had stayed instead of leaving the cabin yesterday? What if she had welcomed him and shown her true feelings when he finally returned, instead of acting like a shrew? What if they honestly and openly talked about what was happening between them? The last thought was the most devastating. Her feelings for Jon left her rocky, but he was only being a man, reacting as any lusty male would to a convenient female.

Just to keep busy she spread her manicure set and a tissue on the table, but the mechanics of doing her nails didn't distract her thoughts from Jon.

They were married, but they were unlike any wedded couple she'd ever known. He wanted her, but what an empty desire it was when his love didn't go with it. Of course he restrained himself. He was counting heavily on a businesslike annulment, uncomplicated by an impetuous affair. He would scorn her if he knew that she'd so quickly switched her love from Bruce to him. How could he think her anything but shallow when she didn't know herself what had come over her? Even though her feelings for Bruce were coming into perspective, she felt nothing but confusion concerning Jon. Love as she'd experienced it with Bruce was fun, exciting, stimulating, but her feeling for Jon brought only pain. Who would have suspected love could hurt so much?

"I'm going out," he said, unexpectedly breaking the tense silence between them.

"It's still pouring."

"I won't melt."

The door thudded shut behind him, but the room was no more comfortable without him, only emptier. At least she didn't have to pretend great interest in filing her nails down to the nubs, as she had unconsciously been doing.

Taking advantage of his absence to slip into her jeans, she did a few exercises, those possible in the confines of the cabin, enjoying it when hard work brought a film of moisture to her upper lip. When exhaustion finally prompted her to stop, she felt more relaxed.

Following Jon's example, she stripped to the waist, but not before she shoved the bolt into place. Scrubbing until her skin glowed pink, she felt more like her own person and even started making plans for dinner. There were cake mixes in the cabinet, and what did she have to lose by trying? Any activity was better than doing nothing.

A German chocolate cake was cooling on the table, and Jon still hadn't returned. She smeared packaged frosting over the somewhat sunken top of the cake, trying to push away little nagging worries. Why should she be concerned about a man who didn't have the courtesy to tell her where he was going or how long he'd be gone? If this was what it was like being married, she couldn't get an annulment quickly enough.

Liar, she accused herself. Liar, liar, liar!

He had to bang on the door to be admitted; she'd forgotten to unbolt it after her sponge bath.

"Why lock it?" he asked. "There's no one here but us."

"I was having a bath."

"So was I," he said grimly, shedding the slicker and taking his towel off its hook to dry his face and hair. "We're getting a year's worth of rain in a few days."

"Wear a hat," she suggested flippantly, "and you won't drip all over the place."

"I can dress myself, thank you."

"Not very well or you wouldn't risk pneumonia running around with a bare head in this weather."

"Wouldn't you love it if you had to rush me down to a hospital?"

He smiled, infuriating her. Did he suspect that she'd considered feigning illness herself?

"You probably don't have enough sense to get sick,"

130

she retorted, unexpectedly using a saying of her great-grandmother's that she hadn't heard in years.

"Homespun wisdom," he said grinning. "You've baked me a cake."

"I have a sweet tooth," she said quickly.

"Don't indulge it too much. It'd be a shame to spoil a beautiful figure."

"It's not your worry."

"No, but I liked that other outfit you were wearing. Why did you change?"

"Jeans are a little more practical in your hideaway."

"And you're always practical?" he challenged.

"I try to be."

"Even when you hopped on a plane to marry a man you hardly knew?"

"Bruce and I spent a lot of time together!"

"Nearly a week by my reckoning. Do you really believe you can learn enough about a person in that length of time to consider marriage?"

"Yes, I do," she said angrily, but it was Jon, not his brother, she was thinking of.

"Maybe," he said, dropping his attack, "but not unless you're a good judge of character."

He took off his shirt and hung it on the now-empty clothes line. When he made no move to put on another, Gina felt herself steaming.

"For goodness sake, get dressed. It's not the middle of summer."

Now she sounded like Grandmother Livingston. What on earth was happening? Jon brought out the very worst in her.

"The inside of that slicker was like a steam bath," he said defensively. "I thought I'd wash first. We're living in pretty close quarters here."

"As if you need to tell me," she snapped. "This is all

131

your design. Why didn't you make this cabin a liveable size?"

"I intended to stay here alone."

"With two double bunks?"

"I like room when I sleep."

"No one can sleep in two beds."

"Occasionally a friend comes with me."

"A friend who doesn't mind cramped quarters?"

"A male friend, for the fishing. No woman I brought here would ever need a separate bunk."

Except me, she thought bitterly.

He did wash in the basin again, then put on a faded gray sweatshirt with cut-off sleeves. Leaving the soapy water on the table, he shook out his sleeping bag on the upper bunk and climbed up with one easy motion.

Resenting the mess he'd left, resenting his easy escape into sleep, resenting his very being, she emptied the water out the door and dried the basin and table. How could such a simple thing as emptying a pan make her so angry? She didn't even know herself anymore!

With a painful flash of self-recognition, she knew she was feeling terribly, terribly sorry for herself. Admitting it was embarrassing; knowing that Jon must sense it was unbearable. It wasn't her way of meeting problems, and she couldn't let it continue.

Jon had ruined her marriage plans with Bruce, but she was honest enough with herself to admit he might actually have done her a favor, saving her from a mistake that could have meant years of unhappiness. She forgave him for tricking her; she couldn't forgive him for letting her fall hopelessly in love with him.

By the time he awoke, she was more composed than she'd been in days. There was nothing to be done about rekindling her love for Bruce, but she would leave Jon very soon, never letting him know how painful it was to do so. She owed that much to her own self-respect.

Tension simmered under the surface, but they got through dinner and the evening by being silently unresponsive, speaking only when necessary, and guarding their bits of space rigorously.

The gentle patter of raindrops dripping onto the roof from a tree put Gina to sleep that night, but not before a long wait listening to Jon's restless tossing. His sleeping habits seemed to have changed since they'd first begun living in the cabin.

The sun had to work to penetrate the moisture-laden haze surrounding the mountain, but by midmorning it succeeded in bathing the clearing in soft yellow light. The saturated logs of the cabin began drying out, ever so slowly, and the air had the heavy pungency of wet mud, decaying needles, and pine resin. It was a heady blend, and they both wanted to be outside in spite of the soggy ground.

Impractical as the idea seemed, hiking greatly appealed to Gina. She wanted very much to take a long, long walk and be revived by the newly washed freshness of the forest.

"Can we go on a hike?" she asked, her enthusiasm giving her voice a lyrical ring.

"You don't mind wet feet?"

"Not a bit!"

"Well, why not? I guess we've both seen enough of the cabin for a while."

He made her wear more clothes than she thought necessary and carry a change of socks, but at last they were ready, sharing a feeling of release like two young children let out of school for vacation.

Leading the way he skirted the edge of the ravine, now watery on the bottom as the surrounding heights drained into it, and headed for higher country.

"You don't mind some hard climbing, do you?" he asked pleasantly.

133

It was a question that didn't need answering; she was ready to follow him anywhere, and he seemed to sense it.

She wanted to make the climb on her own, so she refused his help several times when his hand reached back to give her a boost. The ground was still damp, but she kept her footing by exercising care. They skirted a few puddles, but the mountainous country had its own efficient drainage system, helped along by a brisk but not cold breeze.

For a long time they didn't talk and, in fact, Gina couldn't. All her breath was needed for the increasingly steep climb. Jon often had to wait for her, but his face reflected nothing but relaxed patience and contentment.

The trees thinned out, a blessing since some still let fall drops that dampened their faces and plastered their hair to their heads, her hair a rich brown with a stubborn tendency to curl around her face now that it was damp.

Her breathing was really ragged as she went up a particularly steep incline, and she was fresh out of false pride. When Jon offered her his hand, she willingly let him hoist her the last few feet. They were on a plateau with sparse vegetation, little more than a rocky ledge but overlooking a magnificent vista of rain-washed treetops. The wind whipped at her face, catching strands of hair, making her feel like a recklessly heroic conqueror of peaks.

"It's lovely," she gasped with her little available breath.

"Do you see why I escape here whenever I can?" he asked dreamily, not seeming to direct his question at her.

"Yes, yes, I do."

It wasn't a moment for words, as the warmth of sharing brought them closer together. His arm rested on her shoulders in a companionable gesture, and for the moment it was enough.

"Well," he said, at last breaking the spell, "how about some lunch?"

"I'm famished."

134

By now she was used to his resourcefulness, but she'd never appreciated it more. He spread his ground cloth and took their lunch from his pack.

"Not wine again," she protested feebly, remembering the effect it had had on her the last time they'd picnicked.

"From our winery, of course," he said proudly.

He taught her to roll a small sip of the fruity beverage over her tongue, explaining what the wine tasters expected before they'd approve a vintage. She and Claire sometimes served a bottle of Chianti when they had guests for dinner, but she was far from being a connoisseur. Jon's pleasure in the product of the family winery made her enjoy it, but it was his animation that delighted her. Warm glints danced in his eyes when he was enthusiastic, and his face had a boyish lightness she'd never seen there before. Enjoying himself, he looked more like Bruce in some ways, but less like him in others. There was no self-indulgence in his pleasure, something she now painfully recognized in Bruce's, but Jon did clip off his words the same way his twin did, making it sound as if he were laughing inside at some secret joke.

"If it stays this nice, we'll have some fresh fish tomorrow."

Tomorrow was the word Gina didn't want to hear. Today was all; tomorrow she could safely leave, but she knew it meant leaving her heart behind.

They shared a can of tuna packed in spring water, arranging it on little cracker squares and biting plump olives down to their pits. The salty snack gave them a thirst that was quenched only when the slender green bottle of wine was empty, and Gina felt deliciously light-headed.

"I hope you don't have to carry me back," she said, suppressing an overly girlish giggle.

"If I do, it's my own fault for plying you with spirits."

"Is that what you were doing?"

"Maybe I only want to loosen your tongue."

135

"My tongue!" She did laugh then, a light, trilling sound that echoed back.

"Who were you before my brother bewitched you? Cinderella or Jill going up the hill with Jack?"

"You're being fanciful. I certainly wasn't Cinderella. I adore my parents, and there's no wicked stepmother in my life, only a somewhat rowdy younger brother still in high school."

"And was there a Jack?"

"Not one I tumbled after," she said with a tiny nervous laugh.

"Not until Bruce."

"I wish you wouldn't mention his name in every other sentence," she said uncomfortably.

"He's here with us. I don't see how we can ignore that."

What did he want of her, another avowal of undying love for his brother? She couldn't give him that, but she would never admit her love had shifted so quickly from Bruce to him.

"What about you?" she asked quickly, changing the subject. "I rarely meet bachelors over thirty who are so marriageable."

"Is that how you see me?" He laughed rather harshly.

"Well, it is unusual where I come from."

"I don't think you need my assurances that I'm fond of women," he said with some irritation showing in his voice.

Fond of women! Is that what he called the attraction that was plaguing both of them? She wished she'd never started questioning him.

"I was engaged once," he said with seeming indifference. "It didn't work out. Since Dad's illness I haven't had much time to think about marrying. I've left that to my brother. God knows he's certainly fond of it."

"Who was she?"

"Who?"

"The woman you didn't marry."

"Who didn't marry me. She was my brother's first wife."

His words crackled in the air, as dangerous as the lightning that felled trees and ignited blazing forest fires. Air rushed from her lungs and only a weak *oh* escaped.

"Don't picture me as a tragic Heathcliff," he said quickly. "As it turned out, Bruce did me a favor."

"And now you're doing one for him," she said softly. "Well, you're an artist, a reader of classics, and a farmer. What else is there to know about you?"

"Very little," he said dryly.

"I guess we should go back."

She hugged her arms together, shaking off a chill that seemed to have settled on her.

"Yes. If you were cold, why didn't you say so?"

"Good scout on the trail and all that," she joked half-heartedly.

"That wasn't the reason I married you," he said forcefully.

"What?"

"I can hear the gears grinding in your head. 'Aha,' you're thinking. 'He spirited me away to avenge himself on his brother.' Am I right?"

"You're very wrong. No one thinks like that. You make me sound like the heroine in an old-fashioned melodrama."

"Intentionally, because the idea is too silly for you to waste time considering it. You're here because my brother is squandering family assets on ridiculous marriages. Maybe he'll grow up and take his fun where he can get it without beggaring himself. We're all paying because my father wanted us to have a vested interest in the business instead of depending on him for handouts. Bruce is too rich for his own good, but he won't be if he doesn't kick the marrying habit."

137

"Is that what you think men should do, have fun without committing themselves?"

"Not all men, but my brother, yes."

And you, she thought miserably.

"I'm sure no woman will ever cost you anything," she said angrily.

"No?"

"Let's start back," she insisted, liking their conversation less and less.

"In a few minutes. Let your lunch settle."

"I'm ready now."

"I'm not. I still don't know anything about Gina Livingston."

"There's no reason why you should."

"She's my wife."

"On a piece of worthless paper!"

"Does that mean you're willing to sign the annulment agreement?"

"So that's what this is about, a picnic in the sky while we confess to each other, then sign the agreement."

"You haven't confessed anything."

"Maybe I'm too dull to have a past."

"You are anything but dull! I wish you were."

It was his turn to back off, standing up and walking a few yards away.

"Are you ready now?" she called to his back.

"Very ready," he said, but he didn't move.

She gathered up the empty bottle and other remains of their lunch, stuffing them in his pack along with the ground cloth.

"I'm not your real wife, you know," she challenged him. "I don't see why I should empty your dirty water and pick up after you."

"Is that a wife's job?" he asked, smiling now and walking toward her. "You are an old-fashioned girl."

"I certainly am not. I don't intend to be a slave to my husband."

"Meaning me?"

"Meaning my real husband, when I have one."

"And you still think that will be Bruce?"

So exasperated she wanted to throw something at him, she refused to answer.

The altitude, the wine, the strenuous exercise, all combined to make her feel light-headed, or so she tried to tell herself, denying in her mind that Jon was the cause of her airy feeling of unreality. Twice she asked to rest on the way back, but when they did pause, she was discomforted by his searching gaze and unnerved by his kind solicitude.

"There's no hurry," he said the second time. "I'm going to spread the ground cloth so you can sit awhile."

"It's not necessary. I'm probably just getting a sinus headache from the dampness."

"The first in your life, I'd wager," he said calling her bluff.

It was true. Her mother got sinus headaches, or so she called them. She was borrowing from all her older relatives today. Did that mean they were all part of her, and someday she'd be as absentminded as her maternal grandmother and as poor a driver as her mother? Never mind, she loved them and needed all the help they could give her in dealing with this stranger who'd kidnapped her.

Refusing to rest more than a few minutes, she trailed behind Jon, finding the downhill trek much more difficult than going uphill. She was embarrassed when she fell forward, getting the knees of her jeans muddy and her hands filthy. Jon wanted to clean her hands on his handkerchief, but she wiped them on the sides of her jeans instead. Anything was better than having to be wiped up like an infant by the man she secretly loved.

They were within sight of the cabin when he put his arm around her shoulders.

"You are a good camping buddy," he complimented her. "That was a rough hike, and you never once complained."

"I enjoyed it," she said truthfully.

"So did I."

His smile was warm, and she was too weak to push his arm away. Even a brotherly pat on the back was like a life-sustaining raindrop on her parched garden of love.

"Sorry about your jeans. We can wash again tonight," he said.

It didn't matter, she knew. Tomorrow at the first opportunity, she was leaving. Maybe if he went fishing she could pretend to take a nap. Knowing where the van keys were, she could easily leave. Nothing would interfere with her escape this time.

The full feeling in her throat would go away; she wouldn't always feel like weeping. All the temporary discomforts of her stay on the mountain would be forgotten as soon as she was back with her family and friends.

Jon, you fool, she wanted to cry out, why can't you see that I love you? Why can't you love me?

His arm was still on her shoulders, fitting there, not heavy.

"Poor kid," he said softly, looking at her. "This has been a poor excuse for a honeymoon."

"Jon, let me sign the annulment agreement now."

Abruptly she had realized that when she left, she wanted a copy in her possession. She held her breath, afraid that he'd be suspicious of her request.

"If you'll let me give you what I want to."

"Please, don't make me sign it that way. I don't want to be bought off. I just need to have things settled."

"I won't change the document."

140

"You're insisting on compensation to make yourself feel better, not for me. I don't want your money."

"Then give it to a worthy cause. I'm not trying to tell you what to do with it."

They were in the cabin now, and he moved away, looking at her with a long, level gaze that made her squirm inside.

"Please," she begged.

"If we can't agree on the terms, there's no hurry in signing it."

"It would put my mind at ease."

His face told her that he was remembering the times when the physical attraction between them had been almost irresistible.

"Clean up and change your clothes, then we'll talk about it some more," he said gruffly. When she didn't respond, he left her alone in the cabin.

Looking at her muddy jeans lying in a heap on the floor, she wished she dared burn them. She wanted to leave behind everything that reminded her of the emotional turmoil of being here. When Jon returned, she didn't feel at all up to arguing over the annulment agreement, but she didn't dare leave with their marriage hanging in the air.

"There's no hurry on this," he said as he laid the papers on the table for her to reread. "Why don't you think about it awhile longer?"

"Jon, nothing is going to make me change my mind. You owe me my freedom after the way you tricked me in Las Vegas. Why can't I have it on my own terms, not yours?"

"I'm not used to doing business that way."

She believed it, but desperation made her unwilling to concede defeat.

"This isn't your business; it's my life."

"That's why I want to compensate you. This has been

a very bad experience for you. You deserve some kind of reward."

"I don't want it!"

"Not now, but you're young. Think of what some extra money might mean to your husband or your children someday."

His words tore raw wounds on her heart. Why was he so blind? There would never be a husband in her future. What she felt for him was so special and new and different that her last lingering trace of doubt faded away. Jon was the only man she had ever loved or would ever love. If she'd felt something strong for Bruce, it had only filled the emptiness in her heart until she met her real love.

"How will I know he loves me for myself if I have all that money?" she asked, playing his game for the moment.

"Any man but a total fool would love you for yourself."

His words hung in the air, an offering richer than all his holdings, but she knew they were only tools to bend her to his will. The annulment agreement was becoming a way of settling a contest between them. He insisted on giving her money because it would salve his conscience and because he was used to having his own way. Hadn't he demonstrated that when he ruthlessly deluded his brother's fiancée into marrying him?

"Let me sign it without the money part," she pleaded again.

He only shook his head, looking at her with his lids half shut, lazily assessing the fight left in her.

"I'll put it away for now, but it may be a long winter if you don't change your mind."

"You're bluffing! You have your family's affairs to run. You won't stay here that long."

"Do you want to put it to a test?"

She wanted to say yes, but she was too frightened that he would read more into her challenge than was safe for her. If he ever suspected that she wanted to be with him anyplace and anytime, even if it meant accepting his terms, she would be totally, devastatingly humiliated.

He was folding the agreement, ready to lock it away again, when she grasped at one last chance.

"The amount. Would you change the amount of money?"

His laugh was rich, showing genuine amusement.

"If you weren't trying to get rid of money, I'd say you should be a labor negotiator. You've missed your calling."

"Then you will lower it?"

"How much do you make a year now?"

She told him somewhat shamefully, knowing her salary must seem pitifully small to a man with his resources.

"You're being underpaid, I'm sure. What if I give you what I think you should make for five years?"

"That's still too much," she protested.

"You have to compromise somewhere if we're going to move on this."

Realizing that he was enjoying himself made her angry, but she bit back an antagonistic reply that wouldn't do her cause any good.

"I'm the injured party in this case."

He laughed aloud then.

"Then let me compensate you adequately."

"Money isn't everything."

"But not having it can be very difficult," he said with more understanding than she wanted to hear from him.

"I'm not a charity case. My father is an accountant for a trucking company, and my mother teaches piano and vocal music. We've always made our own way."

"I didn't mean to insult you," he said genuinely contrite. "I need to give you this money more than you need to take it, if you want to know the truth. It isn't easy for me, living with what I've done to you. Maybe if I'd known . . ." His voice trailed off.

"Known what?"

"Known what kind of person you are."

"Then?"

"I would never have tried this. Bruce's last wife was a show girl in Vegas, not very talented except when it came to getting men to pay her bills. I expected you to be her type. Don't look as if I just hit you. But it is the truth."

"I believe you," she said, forcing the words out because he looked so stricken.

"Then let me give you a gift, Gina. Please."

Gifts came in boxes with ribbons and made people happy, Gina thought miserably. No matter how convincing Jon was, the money was still odious to her. If she accepted it, she would hate herself. If she didn't, she would have to leave without any guarantee that their marriage would be annulled. She didn't want Jon to have that power over her. Loving him as she did, only a full and equal partnership could ever make her happy.

With her hand trembling so much she could hardly hold the plastic-enclosed ballpoint, she scrawled her signature below his on three amended copies of the document. At least he had agreed to lower the amount.

"Thank you," he said gently.

"Shouldn't one copy be mine?" she asked hoarsely.

"Of course, here. I wish . . ."

He didn't finish what he was going to say.

To mask her sick sinking feeling, she made a production of putting her copy in her purse. For the rest of the evening they avoided each other's eyes.

CHAPTER EIGHT

She awoke knowing it was her day to leave. Her whole body felt leaden, hardly in any condition to execute a chancy plan, but she lay there rehearsing every move in her mind. She wouldn't back down.

"Good morning." Jon's voice resounded cheerfully across the room, and she was sorry it was too late to pretend to be sleeping.

"Morning."

"I have a pan of date muffins in the oven. If you're awake enough to watch them, I'll go have my dip."

"Are you always a morning person, or is it a curse that only affects you in high altitudes?" she teased lightly, trying to cover the nervousness she felt about her plan.

"Heredity, I think. You won't go back to sleep and burn the muffins?"

"No, I'll get up."

She crawled out of the sleeping bag, wrestling with the long nightgown twisted around her body. Her hair fell over her face, and she pushed it aside impatiently, but in the process of wiggling free, one shoulder strap tore free of her bodice, revealing her full breast, and she knew by the way Jon quickly averted his head that he'd seen.

He stood near the door, tying his robe more securely around his waist and slinging a towel around his neck.

"They should be done in about ten minutes." His voice sounded unnatural.

"What?" she asked, flustered as she clutched her gown against her tingling flesh, remembering too many things in an overpowering flash of recall.

"The muffins. Are you sure you're awake?"

"Yes, I won't let them burn."

It was her cheeks that were burning as she caught a glint in his eyes that his words didn't express. She shuddered in relief when the door closed behind him.

An icy draft had filled the cabin in the moment that the door was open, telling her winter was making threats. How could Jon expose himself to the icy stream when the temperature had to be below freezing? She shivered just thinking of her one bone-chilling dunk.

For a moment she considered rushing to the van while he was bathing, but decided against it. By the time she dressed and got ready to go, he might return. She wasn't going to leave without at least taking her largest suitcase and some of her better clothes. Even after she got off the mountain, she was a long way from home.

She did nearly forget the muffins, but fortunately she rescued them while they could still be called well-browned instead of burnt. By the time she was dressed, they were beginning to cool; she helped herself to one without waiting for Jon.

She fixed orange juice mix for both of them, set out plates, and made her tea, but Jon still hadn't returned. On such a cold morning wouldn't his dip be a very quick one? She hadn't looked at her watch, since time meant very little in the wilderness, but he must have been gone longer than usual.

After drinking her tea with another muffin, she began to feel concern. Another ten minutes passed; surely he must be frozen stiff. Coming out of the water into the frigid air would be torture. Why would he dawdle getting back to the warmth of the cabin?

Worry began gnawing at her. She realized that he could have been delayed going to the stream, but when more time passed without his return, there didn't seem to be any logical reason for his long absence. Wearing only his robe and thongs, he wouldn't wander far from the cabin or do any chores.

Knowing she had no business checking on him, she held back for a few more minutes, but at last she couldn't stand not knowing. He might have slipped and hit his head; he could be lying unconscious. Maybe the icy water had been too much for even a young man's heart.

Slipping into the nylon jacket, she decided to risk the annoyance he'd direct at her if he was perfectly all right. She made her way toward the stream, shivering at the contrast between the warmth of the cabin and the cold, breezy mountain air. From a distance she could see Jon's robe lying on a rock beside the stream, but he wasn't in sight.

Her heart in her throat, she ran, sure that the worst of her fears would be realized; she'd find him lying on the stream bottom, the clear water rushing over his lifeless body. Sheer terror made her look for the thing she dreaded most.

Nothing. He seemed to have disappeared. She didn't see him downstream or upstream, but her heart swelled with relief when she stared at the waterfall. Under the cascade of water she caught just a glimpse of his form straddling huge rocks as the icy torrents bombarded him.

He had to be crazy! It was a cold shower to beat all cold showers. Without thinking she grabbed his robe, towel and thongs, abandoned far from where he was, and raced toward the waterfall.

"Jonathan, you come out of there!" she called frantically over the rumbling noise of the water.

Did he signal? She wasn't sure. He did hesitate, but finally she let him know by gestures that she'd come in if he didn't come out.

Dangling his thongs and towel from her fingers and trying to hold his robe like a shield between them, she tried not to see him move in slow motion toward her. She meant to hold the robe high between them until he slipped into it, but her fingers were stiff from the cold and awkward from holding his other possessions. Just as she sensed he was about to back his arms into the sleeves, the robe escaped her grasp.

He scooped it up and quickly donned it, but she wanted the earth to open up and hide her. He would think she was the worst kind of voyeur, spying on a man in his bath, but her brief glimpse showed her something that troubled her even more than his nakedness. A long, jagged scar, whitened by time but no less disfiguring, traveled down his thigh to his knee, where it was crisscrossed by smaller, neater surgical scars.

Then they were running, his teeth chattering so badly that she could hear the sound from several feet away.

Inside the cabin he calmly shed his wet robe and wrapped up in a blanket, while she frantically shoved a chair near the stove, poured hot coffee, and found a towel to wrap around his soaking hair.

"What on earth were you doing?" she asked, voicing her anxiety.

"It's called a cold shower," he said wryly. "Don't worry. The cold never bothers me much."

"You don't develop polar bear blood living in California."

148

"Honey, I'm okay," he assured her, but the chattering of his teeth belied his words.

Startled by the endearment, she moved away from him, trying to think of some other way to warm him. She held his sleeping bag against the metal of the stove, warming it then turning away while he exchanged it for the blanket.

"You stayed in too long." She scolded him to mask her worry.

"It seemed like a good idea. I guess I was too numb to realize how cold I was. Not smart, I admit."

She knew he was remembering the unfortunate slip of her gown, and a guilty twinge fluttered through her consciousness.

"Did you hurt your leg in an accident?" she asked, wanting to veer away from the reason for his cold shower.

"Depends on what you call an accident," he said, forcing his jaws together to fight the chattering of his teeth.

She thought he wouldn't say more, but eventually he explained. "Bruce was driving too fast, half drunk, and speeded up when I asked him to slow down. We were both lucky, him more so than me."

"You must hate him for it!"

"For a while, when I couldn't play football my senior year in high school." His words came slowly with a lot of chattering. "Would you mind getting me some socks and underwear?"

She found his heaviest wool socks and handed him the items he wanted, going outside briefly while he put them on.

When she looked at him again, huddled by the stove, his unzipped sleeping bag around his shoulders, she was terribly uneasy. His lips were blue, and he was shaking harder than ever. She wanted to shake him herself for staying under the icy waterfall, but she was more worried than angry.

"You're still freezing," she said, feeling helpless.

149

"I can't seem to warm up."

She touched his cheek, finding it clammy and moist in an unhealthy way. It was dangerous to let the body temperature remain below a certain level, she was sure, but the cabin didn't offer many ways of warming up. A hot bath would be perfect, but the biggest kettle in the room only held a couple of gallons. Though, in the absence of heating pads, it might serve as a foot warmer.

Building up the fire to a roaring blaze, she heated a kettle of water to a temperature that was comfortably warm to her touch. Bending down over his protests, she peeled off his socks, alarmed by the coldness of his flesh. Even though he soaked his feet until the water was tepid, he was suffering more than ever, his face gray and his lips still blue. She dried his feet vigorously, but it wasn't enough. She had to get him warm. The contrast between her warm hands and his frigid skin told her what she had to do. She unzipped her sleeping bag and spread it out like a blanket on the bottom bunk.

"Go lie down," she ordered.

"It's warmer by the stove," he said, making a superhuman effort not to let his teeth chatter.

"No, it isn't."

She steeled every fiber of her being to force him to do as she asked. For an instant the silent clash of wills electrified the atmosphere of the cabin, but at this moment she was stronger and more desperate, not knowing what she'd do if something happened to the man she loved.

Stiffly he rose from the chair, moving like a robot toward the lower bunk. He was visibly shaky as she arranged the second sleeping bag on top of him.

Nervously she kicked off her shoes and let her jeans drop to a pile on the floor, then pulled off her shirt and socks, standing for an uneasy moment in her bra and panties before she hurried onto the bunk beside him.

Over his halfhearted protests, she made him squirm

150

out of his T-shirt and socks, knowing she had to warm his flesh with hers as quickly and as thoroughly as possible.

The initial shock came when she wrapped her warm limbs around his and pressed her torso against him. His flesh was so icy against hers that she shivered uncontrollably herself for a short while, then began massaging him with her feet and hands.

"You're crazy," he said hoarsely.

"You have hypothermia, I think," she said in a muffled voice.

"I know my body temperature is too low, but you're still crazy."

She rubbed his face vigorously with both palms, not wanting to enjoy touching him, but unable to deny to herself the effect close contact was having.

It was discouraging; his skin didn't feel any warmer against hers, and he was trembling in spite of his utmost efforts to control it.

Taking one of his hands, she rubbed it frantically on either side, determined to start heat flowing in at least one part of his body.

"No," he said softly. "Don't work so hard. Just let me hold you."

He wrapped his arms around her, cradling her head under his chin, stilling her legs by letting one of his long limbs fall across both of hers.

Slowly, almost imperceptibly, her warmth began to flow into him. His flesh was still cold against hers, but he was still, the convulsive shaking quieted.

"You should leave," he whispered into her hair.

"You're still an iceberg."

"No, I'm much warmer."

Leaning on one elbow he trailed soft kisses over her bare shoulder, then pressed his lips against the veins under the taut skin of her wrist, making the rapid beating of her pulse perceptible to both of them.

151

"You were warned," he said sensuously. "I can't survive another cold shower."

"Never go under that waterfall again," she begged, her voice sounding muffled, the torrent racing through her body making the outside world seem far away and unimportant.

So slowly that it seemed an ordinary thing, he found the clasp of her bra and opened it, letting the scrap of material lie in place while he pressed his lips into the hollow of her neck. Her hands, moving awkwardly over the muscular expanse of his back, couldn't touch him enough. Like a blind person trying to unravel the mystery of a strange object, she pressed hot and eager fingers against his flesh.

Kissing her, he demonstrated that one part of him was very, very warm, his mouth burning against hers. Almost crazed by the intensity of her love, she arched her body under the hot confines of the heavy cover, sure that she could warm him to feverishness with the heat radiated by her need for him.

His beard, long enough now to be soft, brushed the nerve endings in her face until she parted her teeth to receive the deep thrusts of his tongue, not choking as she'd expected, but feeling her restraints slipping away.

With maddening slowness he inched first one strap and then the other off her shoulders until her bra lay freely across her breasts. With a warm breath he blew the garment aside, drinking in the sight for a long moment before he lowered his lips. Teasing her nipples with his tongue, he made her breathless with longing until, finally, he shifted, hovering over her, his body both tender and threatening.

The flesh on his back and hips was still cool to her touch, but he was glowing with internal warmth, throwing off his cold-induced sluggishness as he built a fire between them that not even a roaring torrent of icy water could extinguish.

"You should leave me now," he whispered, but both of them knew the time for that had passed.

Bending over her in his last moment of uncertainty, he smiled, and she knew Jon was all she wanted, all she needed. With a rush of feeling too powerful to resist, she felt a joy so intense yet so compelling that she locked her body against his with a strength born of urgency.

A cry of sheer happiness rang out from his throat as he began a love ballet with his willing but apprehensive partner, taking possession inch by inch, secret place by secret place, slipping off her briefs with fingers that seemed electrified.

Passion sharpened her senses, teaching her things about herself she'd never suspected. Desire had a scent of its own, more devastating than the rarest perfume, and her body had needs beyond the limits of her imagination. Most compelling of all was the need to please, the urge to give happiness to the man who meant everything to her.

She clung to him, pushing aside her mind's warnings and restraints, wanting his fervent kisses and heated caresses, but ready to accept far more.

When she cried out, he became motionless, tenderly kissing her eyelids, beginning again only when her nails dug urgently into his back.

The bridge was crossed, but there was no regret in her backward look. There was only Jon, the man who held her locked in his arms, as unwilling as she was to let this moment in time be gone forever.

Still dizzy with new sensations, she cradled his head on her breasts, mildly shocked when the wetness of his mouth on her nipple sent new sensations coursing downward. She would never, never, never tire of this man!

The force of her emotion made her shiver, and he looked down at her with an expression so intent it was almost frightening. For an instant his face reminded her of his brother, but any thought of Bruce was an unwanted

153

intrusion. She pulled Jon's face to hers and kissed him, daringly exploring the inner recesses of his mouth until he groaned deeply and again became the aggressor.

His words were mumbled and meaningless, soft endearments uttered breathlessly as he took total possession, stroking her flesh until she cried out for release. He had cast away all restraint, and in her eagerness to give, she didn't care, becoming caught up in frenzied sensations until, at last, slippery with passion, they collapsed together.

Gina's first waking sensation was one of warmth. Cuddled against Jon, she delighted in the heat of his body, sure that she had done the right thing; she would never be sorry for having coaxed the fire of life into his too-cold flesh.

Sighing contentedly, she remembered that this was the day she was supposed to leave. The shadows in the interior of the cabin made her guess that it was after noon. Her plan to leave while Jon was fishing seemed to have been made in the remote past.

He moaned slightly and hugged her more tightly, making her a willing prisoner, locked between his arms. She wasn't strong enough to break free of his embrace, and the same was true of his hold on her heart. At that moment she totally lacked the will to leave the cabin, to leave him.

Burrowing her face against the now-comforting warmth of his chest, she let his beard tickle her nose until she suspected he was only pretending to sleep. With a sharp little tug she pulled out a single hair, startling him into revealing his ruse.

"Fiend!" he accused her, seeking revenge with a punishing kiss.

"You were only pretending to be asleep," she accused him between caresses.

"This isn't pretending," he said, locking his mouth over hers, adjusting his body to her contours, awakening sensations she'd thought were too special to reoccur.

"For the first time," he mumbled into her hair, "I think my brother may not be a fool."

Sated, he didn't notice her involuntary stiffening, nor did he see her face, cradled against his shoulder.

Jon thought he'd just made love to his brother's woman, she realized with an angry shock. Everything fit. Jon had good reasons for holding a grudge against his twin; Bruce had caused the accident that had disfigured his leg and spoiled his athletic activities. As if this weren't cause enough for wanting revenge, Jon's brother had also stolen his fiancée. How sweet it must be for the man beside her to know that he was the first man to possess a woman his brother wanted.

Now that the heat of their lovemaking had simmered down, Gina remembered only too clearly every word Jon had said while they lay together. He wanted her, desired her, and thought she was beautiful, but never once had he claimed to love her.

Disappointment swept away all the languid ease her body had felt, and she moved away from Jon even though he reached out lazily to prevent her from leaving.

Moving across the room she was aware of his gaze on her nakedness, so she hurriedly put on her robe, then found the blanket that had served before to curtain the bed. She tucked it under the edge of the upper mattress, even though she heard Jon's soft laughter coming from behind it.

"Isn't it too late to be modest?" he teased her lightly, but he seemed content to lie behind the blanket.

She scrubbed every inch of her body, as though she could wash away the feeling of having been used to further Jon's vengeance against his brother. How could she be such a fool, falling in love with someone whose motives were such a mystery to her? First Bruce, then Jon had made her lose her senses; her recovery from the first had been made easy by her growing love for Jon, but even when she hated him, she couldn't wipe out her feelings for her husband-by-trickery.

Her husband! What had she done? After sacrificing her pride and signing annulment papers that bought her off, she'd blown it. If Jon swore that he had consummated their marriage, the agreement was meaningless. She would have to seek a divorce with all the messiness that entailed. He might even try to block her, knowing that California's community property laws would cost him a great deal. Somehow she would have to convince him to let her go. Would he believe that she wanted absolutely nothing from him except to have her heart back intact?

Grimly she considered her alternatives as she dressed in severe navy slacks and a pale blue oxford cloth blouse. She buttoned it up to her neck, patting down the collar before she began brushing her hair.

She was still going through the motions of brushing her hair when he swept aside the blanket and sat on the edge of the bunk.

"Gina?"

Why did he sound so mellow, so happy? Of course, he was proud of himself. She'd completely forgotten about his brother when she was in his arms. Even if she never saw Jon again, she wouldn't go back to Bruce. That relationship was ruined forever, and he must know it.

"Come here," he ordered softly.

"Aren't you starved?" She hoped her voice didn't sound as unnatural to him as it did to her.

"Sure, but there's no hurry. Sit beside me for a minute."

She didn't want him to crumple her defenses with tender words, but he had a powerful weapon to use against her now: the annulment agreement. She didn't dare risk letting him know that she'd figured out his game of revenge. If he knew how sorry she was for what had happened, he'd be angry. His antagonism could cause her so much misery, she didn't like to think about it.

"Here," she said, taking his robe off the wall hook. "You don't want to get chilled again."

"I do, if you'll promise to warm me again. Come here."

She waited until he stood and belted the robe, then went to him at his insistence.

"Sit down."

She tried to leave space between them, but he spread his thigh against hers and put his arm around her shoulders.

"I don't want you to be sorry for what happened," he said solemnly.

"No, it's all right."

"I'm not used to lukewarm words like all right," he teased, then stopped when he saw that she didn't share his amusement. "Something is wrong."

"No, I just didn't expect it to happen."

"Gina, I didn't want it. I tried every means known to man to make myself indifferent to you, even half-drowning myself in that blasted waterfall. But having you beside me, so warm, so giving. It was too much."

"It was my fault," she said.

"There isn't any fault to pass around," he said heatedly. "It was wonderful, Gina. I've never been happier."

Because you're even with your brother, she thought miserably.

"Look at me," he demanded, cupping her chin in his hand. "If I've done anything to harm you, I'll never forgive myself."

Remembering his insistence on compensating her with money, she felt totally defeated. Of course he didn't want her on his conscience, and now he'd probably insist on making her a rich woman to get rid of her. She detested the thought of what that made her.

"There's nothing to forgive," she said with a tone of false gaiety in her voice that didn't fool either of them. "I'm twenty-four years old. It was time I became a woman."

"You're very much a woman, a lovely one," he crooned, touching her cheek lightly before he brushed her lips with his.

Running his fingers over his own cheek, he smiled rue-fully.

"I've gotten quite a beard. I hope I didn't scratch your face. Does the cut on your face still bother you?"

"No, it's healed, and your beard is soft."

"I'll make a deal," he said. "You fix us a huge lunch or dinner or whatever meal we're on, and I'll scrape off this fur."

"Oh, no," she said quickly. "Don't shave on my account. I like beards."

Originally she'd liked Jon's beard because it made him look different from Bruce. Now she wanted him to keep it for reasons she didn't understand. If he shaved, did it mean he was preparing to make love to her again?

Preparing a meal gave her something to do, and it was late enough in the afternoon to call it dinner. She picked packets at random, and if her selections weren't up to a gourmet's high standards, they sufficed. Both of them ate as though starving, cleaning up a noodle casserole, canned spinach, and an apple dessert.

Time passed slowly that evening. Jon had shaved, but she'd correctly guessed his motive. Looking hauntingly handsome, he didn't bother to dress, lounging with his robe open to the waist in a casual way that said they were a couple now, comfortable together without the need for protective clothing.

She didn't feel that way at all, pulling on a vest before dinner and topping it with a sweater later in the evening, every layer providing more psychological protection against his lingering gaze.

It was plain he expected to share her bed that night, and if he did, she might not be able to deny herself any more than she could refuse him when she was in his arms. They played a time-killing game of gin rummy, but when she lost another fourteen dollars playing for very small stakes, he cancelled her whole debt and refused to play longer.

"I like a challenge when I play," he said, not entirely teasing.

I'm not that anymore, she grimly thought to herself.

Late in the evening she sent him outside on the pretense of hearing a noise, insisting he load his gun and take it with him. He laughed at her, but did it to quiet her anxiety, not knowing he was the cause of it.

By the time he returned, she'd changed for bed.

She zipped up her sleeping bag and threw it against the far wall, slipping inside while he extinguished the lantern. She was still settling down when he hung his robe on a hook and sat on the edge of the bunk.

"Why don't we spread one bag and use the other as a covering, the way you did this morning?" he suggested in a husky voice.

Hating him for reminding her that her action had initiated their lovemaking, she still knew she'd do the same thing again if his life seemed threatened. People died of hypothermia; she'd been sure of it at the time, even if she'd possibly exaggerated the danger.

"I'm really tired," she said, yawning realistically.

"Of course you are, darling."

He leaned over and kissed her ear, then, not satisfied, found her mouth and claimed it for one long, lingering kiss.

"Sleep well, sweetheart," he whispered.

The bunk creaked as he got into his sleeping bag, but his restlessness wasn't what kept her awake that night. He fell asleep quickly, spreading out over the bed so his hand rested near her face. She meant to push it away, but the firm texture of his fingers felt warm and wonderful to her touch, and she held them to her cheek for a long time, finally moving his whole arm away only because her heart was breaking.

This was the last night she would lie sleepless, breathing in rhythm to his every breath, wishing she was in his arms, knowing he'd never truly be hers.

Her pillow was damp before she finally dropped into a fitful sleep.

CHAPTER NINE

Why was he sleeping so soundly and so late? Lying rigid and wide awake in her sleeping bag, Gina felt trapped. With the log wall on one side, Jon on the other, and the plank slats on either end, there was no escape from the bunk without crawling over him, a move that would surely wake him. Lying still was a torture, and her eyes felt dry and stinging, as though she'd forced them open in a sandstorm.

Her heart nearly stopped when he shifted his position, crowding her against the wall with his still-sleeping face turned in her direction. Lying so close to him, she could see the slight redness under his chin line where shaving his heavy beard had scraped the skin. His firm cheek had only an early hint of dark bristles and, against her will, she wondered how his face would feel against hers now that it was smooth and soft.

As though reading her thoughts, he slowly opened his eyes and regarded her with pleasure, catching one of her hands in his and bringing her palm to his cheek.

"Been awake long?" he drawled.

"No, I just woke up," she lied, not wanting him to

suspect that she'd lain sleepless for hours doing nothing but thinking of him.

"You look wide awake."

There wasn't any answer to that, not that he gave her a chance. His good-morning kiss was firm and demanding, sending nervous tremors down her spine. She shuddered and, mistaking her reaction, he moved closer and bundled her into his arms, sleeping bag and all.

"Mornings are getting colder," he said.

"Promise me you won't go into the stream again," she said urgently.

"You have my promise." He nibbled her ear possessively and whispered, "I don't need to."

His unspoken message filled her with alarm; he was expecting something she couldn't give. Knowing that she was only a pawn in his game with Bruce cheapened everything that had happened between them. If only once he'd sworn that he loved her for herself, passionately and fully, he could claim her body and soul. Lacking that, any relationship between them was doomed to frustration and failure.

Why couldn't it have been Jon she'd met first? Bruce was too wrapped up in his own concerns to interfere in his brother's personal life; he wouldn't put himself out to avenge wrongs that happened in the past. Jon would; intense, serious, sensitive, he saw the world as a ledger book, collecting debts owed as rigorously as he paid those he incurred. His balance sheet would always be in order.

"Will you start a fire in the stove?" she asked.

"I had another way of warming up in mind."

"Please, Jon."

He leaned over her, intently studying her face.

"Are you trying to put me off?"

His hand located the tab of the zipper and slowly pulled it downward until her sleeping bag was open to her thighs. Peeling it back he began stroking the lower part of her

162

breasts, teasing her by avoiding the tips that strained against the filmy fabric of her gown.

"Jon, no," she cried out, her voice made harsh by her own inner struggle.

"Are you all right?"

His words, tender and caring, lashed at her resolve.

"Yes, I just want to get up."

He moved aside to let her go, not commenting when she again hung the blanket to cut off his view of the room. As quickly as she could, she pulled on some clothes and went outside.

The wind whipped at her, making itself felt through the jacket, but she stayed out a long time, wandering in the clearing until her footsteps made a new path on the frosted ground. Her instinct was to leave immediately; she knew where the van key was, and the odds of her getting away were better than even. Still, she wasn't a gambler; she wanted a sure thing. Jon would certainly try for some fish today, and she'd be able to leave, taking her purse and a suitcase with her. It would be sheer foolishness to leave the mountain without taking coins for the phone. When Jon called to her from the cabin door she felt calmer, resolved that she would leave him before he suspected the truth, that she loved him desperately.

"Breakfast's ready," he said cheerfully when she stepped into the room. "For a girl who was cold, you spent a long time out in that wind."

"Woman."

"What?"

"Yesterday you called me a woman, not a girl."

"Of course," he said, grinning. "All woman."

He'd outdone himself fixing the best breakfast that the cabin's supplies allowed, sacrificing the last of their fresh eggs on an omelet with bits of sausage, onion, and cheese. She ate her full share, not knowing how great the distance was to the nearest restaurant or grocery store nor how long she would have to wait for a chance to leave unseen.

They worked together doing the morning chores, and Jon was never far from her side. His good mood was contagious, serving to remind her of how much she'd miss him. In this light-hearted mood he was charming, witty, considerate, more like Bruce than ever before. Was she a hopeless idiot for switching her love from one brother to the other so quickly, or was she simply bewitched by the inherent masculinity that was so much a part of both?

This is where her rashness had led, to a wilderness cabin and the companionship of a man she loved beyond reason and hope. By making such a hasty decision to marry, she had hurt Bruce and perhaps Jon too. Certainly his pride, if nothing else, would be wounded when he learned of her flight from the mountain. How much better it would have been to follow a slower, saner course after meeting Bruce and not expose herself to the consequences of an impulsive act. For once in her life she'd done something totally unexpected and unreasonable, and her heart would never recover.

Yet loving Jon made it seem worthwhile, and for a few wild moments she was tempted to stay with him until he forced her to go. Only her pride held her back. Jon meant far too much to her; as much as she'd suffer by leaving him, it was nothing compared to the pain of being cast aside when his revenge on Bruce was complete.

"You're far away," he said, coming up behind her unexpectedly as she rolled up her sleeping bag for the day.

"Just thinking, I guess," she said, trying to sound carefree.

"I'd like to know what you're thinking."

"Nothing very deep or significant."

"Share it with me."

Too rattled by his closeness to think fast, she stammered out the first thing that came into her head.

164

"My parents will wonder where I am all this time."

"Are you telling me you're standing here with me beside this bed, miles from the nearest human, and you're worrying about your parents? You're not a child, Gina."

"Then don't patronize me."

"I'm not. I just want you totally here with me, not miles away in your mind."

"You've made sure I stay here with you."

"You have a right to resent that," he said unhappily, "but I don't think things are the same as they were."

"Nothing's changed."

"This has."

He drew her into his arms, pressing her so close she couldn't catch her breath, kissing her with a thoroughness that made her quiver down to her toes. With a grip just short of hurting, he kept her captive in his arms, his insistence making her senses swim.

There was no taking back what had happened, she reasoned on the fringe of surrender. What harm could there be in submitting to his lovemaking when her needs were just as great as his, swelling within her as Jon's embrace showed an urgency that was contagious.

With a sudden, unnerving shift from forcefulness to tenderness, he trailed his lips across her forehead and kissed both eyelids, letting her lashes play across the tip of his nose.

Unbuttoning her blouse with maddening slowness, he gently tugged it loose from the waist band of her slacks. Expecting a fevered assault on her breasts, she tensed, letting her hands fall limply to her side. Instead he captured all her fingers and brought them to his lips, kissing each one in turn until she felt he was paying her homage, as though she were a queen and he an adoring subject. She couldn't resist because there was nothing to resist.

Pulling her onto his lap, he sat on the edge of the bunk kissing her lightly but not without effect. Tremors of sheer joy coursed down her back as she parted her lips to receive the fullest and sweetest kiss of her life. How unfair, she thought, that one man possessed this power to squeeze the last drop of delight from her body, turning her will to water as he carried her to new heights of sheer yearning.

"Tell me Bruce never made you feel like this," he pleaded.

More surely than the icy torrents of the waterfall could, his words washed away her passionate longings.

"That's all you care about," she cried out, escaping from his arms and backing away from him. "Taking Bruce's place!"

"Do you think I want you in my arms thinking of Bruce?" he said angrily. "Don't you think I know you can look at me and see my brother's face? Am I so wrong to want to know if you're with me, not him?"

"Does it matter? You've had your revenge on Bruce. Never mind that you've ruined my life doing it!"

"Revenge? What are you talking about?"

"At least don't pretend with me!" All her stored-up resentment poured out as she challenged him. "You're getting even with Bruce, regardless of the consequences."

"Is that what you think? That I married you, brought you here, just to get even with my brother?"

"He caused the accident that kept you from playing football. He married the woman you were engaged to."

"And you think I brought you here because of things that happened years ago? Don't you believe a word I've told you?"

The color drained from his face, making his eyes darker and more threatening. The anger that burned in them made Gina tremble, more afraid than angry now as his gaze forced her to inch farther away.

"Answer me!" he demanded furiously. "If you don't believe me, why did you let me make love to you?"

There was no answer she could give him. He slammed

his fist against the support post of the bunks, the forceful blow resounding in the limited confines of the cabin. Seeing a small trickle of blood on his knuckles, Gina felt as though her vocal cords had swollen shut.

"You're bleeding," she finally managed to whisper.

"Yes, I'm bleeding."

His voice was flat and hard, and she wondered if he'd hit the post to keep from hitting her. Furious now herself because he seemed to be casting blame on her, she didn't try to hold back her doubts.

"Now we can't get an annulment!"

"So that's the whole thing behind it. I knew you were cold to me this morning, but I was fool enough to believe you were just getting over the shock of making love for the first time. I even blamed myself for taking advantage of you. Can you believe that? I thought my brother'd found an innocent girl just because you'd never been to bed with a man before."

"Don't throw it in my face."

"I'm not. Until a few minutes ago I thought it was wonderful, as though yesterday was something special."

"Because you had what Bruce wanted!"

"Because I thought you were giving me a cherished gift."

"It never would have happened if you'd let me go. Wasn't it enough that you ruined my wedding and made Bruce think I stood him up? Why did you have to bring me here and keep me prisoner?"

"You won't have any reason to complain, will you? I knew no woman of Bruce's would refuse money, but I didn't think you'd go for the jugular."

"What do you mean?" Her hands were trembling so badly she clenched them behind her back so Jon wouldn't see them.

"Don't pretend!"

He reached under the bunk and pulled out the metal box, fumbling with the key around his neck to unlock it.

"Here, two sets of worthless paper."

He tore the annulment agreement and its duplicate into shreds, tossing the scraps into the air. They floated for a long second, then scattered on the floor like the confetti that had been missing at their wedding.

"I still have my copy," she said defiantly.

"Yes, in your purse."

In three steps he reached the cabinet where she'd left it, dumping it upside down so the contents spilled across the floor, her lipstick mirror shattering with more noise than its size warranted.

"Here! At least I'll never have to sit in court and hear how I repeatedly ravaged you. You win, Gina. The annulment is null and void. You can go for the big payoff."

"That isn't what I want!"

Crying now, she couldn't look at his face as the full realization of what he was saying hit her. He thought she was after a divorce instead of an annulment. The pain of hearing him accuse her of wanting half of his wealth was unbearable.

She ran from the cabin, thinking only of the van and escape. Too agitated to even notice the cold, she slipped, slid, and nearly fell down the incline toward the van, praying that the key was still hidden in the same spot.

With her eyes so full she could hardly see, she stopped to grope for the bit of metal that would take her away from the nightmare of Jon's anger.

"So you know where the key is!"

His words were more biting than the mountain wind, and his voice was arctic-cold. The expression on his face made her freeze, her hand suspended in air.

"You could have left," he said, "but that didn't suit your plans, did it? You had to be sure you didn't leave here a virgin; otherwise I might hold you to the annulment."

"You are so wrong!" she said bitterly.

"Then why are you still here?"

Everything that had happened blurred in her mind, and she didn't know how to answer without telling Jon the truth, that she'd delayed leaving because, in her weakness, she loved him too much.

"I was going. The day you went under the waterfall. Never had a chance." Her words came in disjointed spurts as she forced her legs to straighten, unable to bear having Jon towering over her, his face contorted by fury.

"You can go," he said, his words biting into her consciousness like the fangs of a rattler. "Come back to the cabin and get all of your things. I don't want so much as a hairpin left to remind me you were ever here."

"I don't wear hairpins," she said, trying to rally some kind of defense against the damning accusations he was making.

Then she knew. It was a smoke screen. By putting her in the wrong, he was distracting her from his own underhanded motives. He'd brought her here to spite his brother, and making love to her had been the culmination of his revenge against Bruce. He hadn't worried about the annulment when he took his brother's woman to bed.

"You must really hate your brother," she cried out to him as he climbed ahead of her.

Turning to face her, his face was an unreadable mask. "Believe what you like if it salves your conscience."

Throwing her possessions into her suitcases with no pretense at order, he neither looked at her or spoke to her.

"I'll pack my own things," she said angrily.

"No, I want you out of here immediately. I don't want to see you or hear from you again until our lawyers have all the terms of the divorce worked out. Then I trust our meeting will be quick and businesslike."

Now that he'd said the word aloud, Gina felt she'd reached the depths of despair. Jon was casting her off as if they'd never given themselves to each other, as if their bodies had never carried them to the unbelievable heights of pleasure. The truth of his feelings for her was the bitterest pill she had to swallow. He'd casually used her body because she was a woman. His heart and mind had always been closed to her.

"You can send me away, Jonathan, but the divorce is your worry. You arranged this marriage; you can arrange the divorce. And whether you believe it or not, I won't accept a penny of your filthy money. Seeing what it's done to you, I don't want to be contaminated by it."

"You know you're safe making pretty speeches because the laws of the State of California and a good divorce lawyer will do your dirty work for you."

"Just remember," she said furiously, "you tricked me into marrying you."

"Of course, I remember. The only satisfaction I have is that your marriage fling with Bruce would have been more enjoyable for you. But don't worry, Gina. You'll be a richer woman than you suspect." A new note crept into his voice, both puzzling and depressing. "I'll see that you're taken care of."

The resignation in his voice was more crushing than his anger had been. A man who ranted and raved might care just a little. If he was as indifferent as his last words sounded, she meant absolutely nothing to him.

Hurting so badly she didn't know if she could reach the van, let alone drive it, she watched woodenly as he left with two of her suitcases, expecting her to follow with the odds and ends left behind. Her feet seemed rooted to the floor, and only the sharpness of his voice when he returned roused her to move.

Leaving this way was wrong, terribly wrong. There must be some words that could heal the rift between them, some way of taking them back to yesterday and the moments when their whole world was each other. One glance

170

at his face, dark, sullen, withdrawn, told her it was too late. There would never be anything between them in the future because the past had been a cruel farce, a game that pitted brother against brother for possession of her. Only somehow she had managed to steal a prize herself, a hold on the precious Kenyon wealth. Finding that his plan had backfired, Jon had created a wall of anger and hatred between them.

"You'll want to call Bruce," he said, forcing all expression from his voice. "I'll write down our number at the ranch and the name of the hotel where he usually stays in Las Vegas. You might try the latter first."

Nodding dumbly, she took the slip of paper in a shaky hand.

"You can't get lost," he went on. "Just follow the road until you get to a general store and gas station. You can make your calls from the pay phone there, and they'll give you directions to wherever you want to go. There's a small town about a two-hour drive from there where you can have lunch."

There were no words of thanks at her command. How could she show gratitude to a man who had just shattered all her hopes and rejected her love without recognizing that it existed?

"There's no reason to hope you'll do anything for me, I suppose, but I also wrote my attorney's name and number on that paper, Steve Garcia. If you'd let him know I'm stranded here, I'd appreciate it."

"I'll let him know," she said stiffly.

She didn't want revenge; seeing what it had led Jon to do was too terrible even to contemplate it herself. She didn't intend to take his van any farther than necessary, though. As soon as she could find a bus station or a car rental, she'd hire someone to drive it back to him. There was no point in telling him, however. The less conversation they had, the better the chance that she wouldn't break down before they parted.

Seeing her to the van with the rest of her possessions, he was silent, not even glancing her way. If he noticed when she brushed away a particularly persistent tear, he gave no sign.

The keys were in his possession for only an instant; he handed them to her, being careful not to let their fingers touch. Following her to the door on the driver's side, he finally spoke. "Take this money. You'll need it to get home."

This time he did touch her hand, pressing a wad of bills against her palm and locking her fingers around them when she tried to refuse his offering.

"I don't want your money."

"Take it anyway," he said harshly. "How do you expect to buy gas and make phone calls?"

"Did it ever occur to you that I have money of my own?"

"Not enough for a plane ticket to Chicago."

"You looked in my purse!"

"Yes." There was no apology in his tone.

"You are the most overbearing, insufferable human being I've ever met!"

"Call me names if it pleases you."

Furious, she sent the money flying away toward the drop-off above the ravine, but it was too far away. The light bills scattered instead of going over the edge, most of them dropping to the ground where they could be easily retrieved.

"How the hell do you think you're going to get all the way home with the money you have?" he asked angrily.

"I'll manage without yours!"

"I'm warning you, Gina. You can't depend on Bruce. You may find he's otherwise occupied when you get to Vegas."

172

"That's the final straw! You steal your brother's wife, malign him, and try to make me believe one week will make him forget me. Isn't there any limit to what you'll do?"

She started to climb into the van, but he held her back, his hold on her arm too firm to break free.

"Let me go!"

"Not until you pick up every single bill and put them in your purse."

"It's your money. You pick it up!"

So frustrated that tears were welling up in her eyes, she stood her ground.

"I'm not letting you go without it."

"Easing your conscience again?" she asked, fumbling for a tissue. "I wish you were a pauper!"

His answer was lost as she sobbed, hating herself for losing control. She hardly noticed when he took the keys from her hand, but she was aware that he gathered up the bills one by one, reaching inside the van when he'd found all he could.

"They're in the glove compartment," he said. "You made the grand gesture and threw them in my face. Now be sensible and use them if necessary."

Standing so close that she felt suffocated by his nearness, he spoke softly now. "Are you all right? Can you drive the van?"

His concern hurt more than his anger at this point. For one panicky instant she thought he'd touch her.

"I'm fine. I'm leaving," she blurted out through her tears.

"Take it easy going downhill," he warned. "Keep it in low gear on the steeper grades. Go slow; I haven't had a chance to check all the way for washouts."

"Stop sounding like my mother!"

They came together, his arms encircling her, holding

173

her against him, but even when his lips descended on hers, their separate pains made the kiss bittersweet.

Nothing changed; they drew apart, both wanting to say something, but the words hung between them unsaid.

"Be careful," he warned when she was behind the wheel, unable to close the door because his body blocked it.

Careful, cautious, conservative, the three big words that would again rule her life from now on. She'd always been the one who wouldn't cross the street against the light or try to fake her way into a movie on a child's ticket. The one reckless chance in her whole life had been fated to yield nothing but heartbreak; never again would anyone have to warn her about the dangers of taking risks.

The only stick-shift car she'd ever driven was her brother's, an aging model that barely repaid him for the care and attention he lavished on it. Highly critical of her shifting, he discouraged her use of it. Fortunately she knew enough to use the clutch, easing the van into first and edging away from the clearing. She didn't look back. If Jon looked upset about her handling of his vehicle, she might be tempted to roar away in a shower of loose dirt and stones. *Careful, cautious, conservative,* the words went through her mind.

As soon as she was well out of Jon's sight, she stopped the van and indulged in a full scale cry, weeping until her tissue supply was exhausted and her head was pounding.

Either the road had suffered from the fall storms or her driving wasn't as adequate as Jon's; the van bounced, slithered, and shook on the rugged surface, requiring so much effort just to stay upright on course that she had to give it her full attention. At least there was no way to get lost, no side roads or forks to confuse her. If only life were so straightforward!

174

CHAPTER TEN

The service station and general store appeared sooner than she'd expected. Had Jon exaggerated the isolation of the cabin to discourage her from leaving? If so, that was one thing she could forgive him; the distance was still too great to cover on foot without proper hiking gear and experience.

A rambling, shingled building housed the store and living quarters, while two antiquated gas pumps sat on a small island of concrete surrounded by rutted dirt. A huge, crudely lettered sign announced SELF-SERVICE ONLY.

The gas gauge didn't register anywhere near empty, but for her own peace of mind, Gina wanted to fill the tank. Since she didn't own a car, the procedure for refueling was largely a mystery. Fumbling with the key to unlock the gas tank, learning how to pump gas from the nozzle, and wondering when to stop to avoid an overflow took more time than she wanted to waste, but there was no real reason for hurrying. It was still morning and, if she was honest with herself, she had to admit there was no place she wanted to be except back on the mountain with Jon.

A faded, middle-aged woman, her long, lank hair tied back in a tail, took Gina's money for the gas and somewhat reluctantly changed a ten-dollar bill to give her coins for the phone.

The pay phone was by the door, out in the open without any enclosure. Aware of the woman's eyes curiously following her, Gina changed her mind about calling from the store. Instead, to atone for the handful of unused coins, she bought a day-old newspaper and a plastic holder of mints.

The directions to the nearest town, extracted from the clerk in the store, were simple enough—just follow the road and ignore any cutoffs. Although she was beginning to feel more comfortable handling the van, Gina drove slowly, trying to decide what to say and do when she reached the town. Contacting Bruce was her first priority, but she knew a call to her parents was necessary too. In spite of Jon's telegram, or maybe even because of it, they were sure to be anxious about the whereabouts of their only daughter.

The town wasn't much more impressive than the general store had been, a small community kept alive by lumber interests in the area and the trade of summer campers and hikers. All the businesses were clustered on one street, the first paved road on Gina's trip from the mountain, with residences situated on short streets running at right angles to this thoroughfare. A lumber yard surrounded by a yellow plank fence faded with age was the first building on the street, and a few blocks farther the town ended abruptly at the entrance to a group of tiny tourist cabins. Wanting privacy more than anything else, she decided it might be worthwhile to rent a cabin for the day, if there were phones there.

The young man behind the registration desk had a face flaming with acne and more questions than answers, seeming to feel that his role as official town welcomer required

176

him to screen all visitors. Inventing a story about working for a real estate investment firm, Gina finally persuaded the desk clerk to take her money ánd supply her with a key.

"Cabin number three. It's got the best view," he said proudly.

The interior made Jon's cabin seem roomy, but a heavy black phone beside the chenille-covered bed was all Gina saw. At last she could make contact with the world she'd left behind, and maybe, just maybe, the love and concern of her family would help fill the awful, aching void, not that anything could erase the pain of her love for Jon.

Catching her father home for lunch, she talked to both parents, assuring them that she was fine.

"Things didn't work out quite the way I expected," she said vaguely, sidestepping most of her mother's anxious questions.

"Are you coming home now, dear?"

"No, not for a while."

Gina didn't know why she said this; until the moment her mother asked, she hadn't considered doing anything else. Now the prospect of being overwhelmed by their understanding and concern seemed stifling. She wasn't sure if she ever wanted to return to Illinois.

"What happened to *careful, cautious,* and *conservative?*" she asked herself aloud after ending her call home.

Impulsively she'd just decided what she wasn't going to do: return to her safe, orderly, dull life and a job that was little more than that of an errand girl. But what on earth was she going to do? Unless she spent Jon's money, which she had no intention of doing, she could live for about a week on what she had with her. That didn't allow much time to plan the momentous changes in her life.

Much more nervously she dialed Las Vegas information and obtained the number of the hotel written on the slip of paper Jon had given her. What could she say to the man

177

she'd jilted, however unintentionally? How could she explain marrying Jon by mistake? Would Bruce be too furious to listen? Did he react to disappointment the same way his twin did?

By now it was noon, and she hoped Bruce wouldn't be hard to locate. She'd rented the cabin to conduct her calls in privacy, a luxury she could ill afford, but the prospect of spending a night alone in the gray-walled little hovel was singularly unappealing. She planned first to take a nap to calm and relax herself, have an early dinner, then drive to wherever she was going. The fact that she didn't have a destination made her feel as if butterflies with frosted wings were having a convention in her midsection. Maybe she could drive Jon's van to Las Vegas and leave it in Bruce's care. Let him be responsible for getting his brother down from the mountain.

The hotel quickly confirmed that Bruce Kenyon was a guest, connecting her to his room with speedy efficiency. Counting the rings, she waited the usual six, but the need to put her past in order made her reluctant to hang up. Bruce might be in the shower or out on a balcony, if there was one. At last her persistence was rewarded when a sleepy voice mumbled "Yeah."

"Bruce?"

"Yeah."

"This is Gina."

For a long moment she wasn't sure if he'd fallen asleep or was refusing to talk to her.

"I didn't expect to hear from you." Sleepiness was replaced by sullenness.

"I have to tell you what happened."

"You changed your mind. I know that already."

She spoke quickly, afraid that he'd hang up; she couldn't really blame him if he did.

"No, it wasn't that way. I got a telegram telling me to meet you a day early."

178

"The hell you did," he snapped.

"Just listen, please, Bruce! I took the plane earlier, and I thought you met me."

"You're not making sense."

"Jon met me. Your brother."

"I know he's my brother," he said impatiently, "but what's this about him meeting you?"

"Bruce, I thought Jon was you. I married him!"

The silence on the phone lasted so long, she was forced to speak again. "Jon married me, pretending to be you, so you wouldn't get married for the third time and lose all your land if we ever got a divorce."

"You're actually married to Jon?"

"Yes."

No reaction could have surprised her more than the boisterous laughter that flooded her ear from the phone.

"Bruce, it's not a joke! I'm really married to Jon."

"I don't doubt it in the least. I just can't believe he'd go that far to play big brother."

"He isn't playing anything. He was going to make me stay in a mountain cabin until your cruise started."

"Where are you now?"

"In a little town in Arizona."

"Why did he let you go?"

"It's a long story. It doesn't matter now. Bruce, aren't you upset that your brother married me just to get even with you?"

"To get even with me for what?"

"For the accident, his leg. For marrying his fiancée!"

"Gina, are you all right? You're talking nonsense."

"We are married!"

"Yes, yes, I believe that part. Jon's been trying to keep me out of trouble for so many years, I don't doubt he'd try something drastic to save me from another messy divorce."

"You never told me about your second marriage," she accused him, wondering why she didn't feel angry.

"Honey, I was sure you and I were something special. Why load all my old problems on you?"

His answer didn't surprise her. Somehow she felt that she knew Bruce better now than she had before she'd flown to Las Vegas to marry him.

"It doesn't matter now, but I don't know how you can be so calm when Jon did this just to get revenge."

"What gave you that idea?"

"I . . . I just figured it out."

"Gina, you'd better refigure. You just don't know Jon. He was the one who talked Dad out of sending me to a military academy after the accident. If he couldn't play football, he wanted to be damn sure I upheld the family honor. I did, too. I worked my butt off making all-state because I owed it to Jon."

"But you married Jon's fiancée," she argued.

"I got stuck with her, you mean. She wanted Kenyon money, and it didn't matter which brother she hooked. Only I was dumber. Jon was so glad he hadn't made that mistake, he even helped with the divorce expenses."

"I don't understand," she said weakly, hearing her own heart pounding in her ears.

"This marriage of yours and Jon's, it's not for real?" he asked.

"No, not for real," she answered miserably.

"Look, sweetheart, we can still have our honeymoon before I leave and worry about getting married after my cruise. Do you have wheels?"

"Jon's van, but, Bruce . . ."

"No *buts!* We had a little delay, that's all. I don't know why Jon changed his mind about keeping you away from me, but I'm sure going to take advantage of it. Nothing's changed, has it? Look, darling, we have enough days left to do the town and make up for lost time."

"Bruce!"

"Hey, Gina, it doesn't matter. Jon thought I was marrying another show girl type or something. If he let you call me, he must approve of you. We'll have everything but the ceremony, and I promise we'll get married as soon as you're free and I'm back. Is Jon going to annul the marriage?"

"Bruce, things have changed," she said desperately. "I only called because I wanted you to know I didn't stand you up."

"So?"

"I'm not coming to Las Vegas. It wouldn't work with us, Bruce. I'm sorry, I'm really sorry."

"I see." His voice was hard.

"I really cared, Bruce, but we just didn't know each other well enough to get married. It would have been a mistake. I'm not right for you."

"I get the message. Well, lose a wife, gain a sister-in-law," he said harshly.

"No, it's not that way!"

"I don't give a damn how it is. Good-bye, Gina."

The phone went dead in her ear. She hadn't had a chance to mention bringing the van to Las Vegas.

Bruce had nothing but admiration for his brother; the idea that Jon wanted to get even for past injuries seemed ridiculous to him. She was a fool, but not because she'd acted impulsively when her heart told her what to do. Just the opposite! By listening to logic instead of her feelings, she'd given up her chance for love without even a fight.

Tossing the cabin key on the desk in front of the startled young man, she demanded that he tally up her phone bill, then burned with impatience while he prepared it. Rushing out to the van, her head was swimming with plans. First she had some very important purchases to make.

The owner of the hardware store shook his head skeptically, doubting that the item she wanted was available

181

anywhere in the area. Too excited to give up, she raced across the street to the variety store where, inspired by a display of children's toys in the window, she knew the answer. She had to send a reluctant clerk into the storeroom, but when she emerged from the store, she felt triumphant.

A couple of small purchases rounded off her shopping needs, then she saved herself time by remembering that banks almost always had a notary public on the premises. The size of the local bank matched that of the town—a two-cage operation with only one teller on duty, and the president himself was visible to the public at his desk blocked off from the rest of the room by a low rail.

Gina tried the teller first and ended up at the president's desk. He seemed to consider her request below his dignity, but when she offered to do the typing herself, making it sound like a matter of life and death, he finally relented, even refusing to accept the usual notary's fee. With the easy parts of her plan completed, she hurried back to the van, her stomach grumbling from a combination of nervousness and simple hunger. The latter she could do something about.

The town's sole café was nearly empty; the lunch hour rush was over, and the one very young waitress was more interested in making time for her own noon meal than in waiting on one more customer, especially an out-of-town woman.

Sensing the girl's languid unwillingness, Gina asked, "What's the quickest thing you can bring me?"

"There's some macaroni and cheese left from the noon special."

"Fine, and a glass of milk."

The pasta had turned rubbery and the cheese had about as much taste as cardboard, but Gina ate quickly and mechanically to still the growling of her stomach.

Outside the sun hardly warmed her cheeks, and she was

reminded of how short the fall days were becoming. The last thing she wanted was to drive over half-eroded roads in the dark.

Inside the van, headed in the right direction, she tried to calm down by breathing deeply. Even though she knew exactly what she was going to do, she couldn't believe this was Gina Livingston, the woman who'd been reluctant to risk a dollar in a slot machine. Now she was staking her life's happiness on a far more reckless gamble.

Was going uphill always slower, or did she only imagine that the trip was taking ten times as long as it should? She passed the isolated general store at last, grateful that the capacity of the van's tank allowed her to skip this stop.

Her hands had been gripping the steering wheel so tightly that her fingers ached; she flexed first one hand, then the other, knowing that the hardest part of the drive was ahead of her on the steep incline.

More used to the van now, she didn't have any real difficulty staying on the road, but the sameness of the woods made her feel like she was on a treadmill, always short of her destination because some giant wheel was moving the road backward as she drove forward.

The clearing was like a bit of paradise when she finally reached it, parking without bothering to maneuver the van around into a position facing back downhill. On the first trip to the cabin, she carried her purchases and her purse with the notarized document safely inside. Her heart soared with relief when she saw that Jon was nowhere in sight. Praying that he'd be gone long enough, she hurried back to the van and dragged out the suitcase she needed.

The cabin was familiar in a way that made her want to weep, a lingering scent of fried fish, fragrant coffee, and hard yellow soap all combining in a special way to tease her nostrils with memories of the many things that had happened here. The fire in the stove was only a glowing ember, but all the pails and pans were full of stream water.

183

Jon must have wanted to save the replenished cistern water for emergencies.

One thing was different. Jon had added a decorative touch to the cabin in her absence. Nailed on the inside of the door was the sketch he'd drawn of her, the nude study she'd objected to. He'd only pretended to burn it; the page he'd thrown into the fire must have been a substitute.

Why had he put her picture on the door, the only flat wall space in the room? Her heart pounded wildly, wondering if he'd hung it there because it was a picture of her or because he was proud of his talent. She didn't dare hope for the first.

Gina's first task was to heat water, lots of water, which she did while she made her other preparations, running to the door every few minutes to see if Jon was coming. The early sunset made the interior of the cabin dusky, and she lit the lantern, pacing restlessly once the last of her work was done.

That she saw him minutes before he came inside was sheer good fortune. With desperate haste she began emptying the steaming kettles, swishing her hand frantically to combine hot and cold water made fragrant by the best bubble bath she'd been able to buy in the small town. He found her that way, on her knees.

"Gina!"

"I've brought you a present," she said nervously.

"A kid's wading pool?" He sounded incredulous.

"It was the closest thing to a portable bathtub I could come up with on short notice."

"What the devil are you doing back here?"

He wasn't making it easy for her. Clearing her throat, she tried to remember all the carefully thought-out things she'd planned to say. Something entirely different popped into her mind.

"Have you read the story about the lady and the tiger?" she blurted out.

184

"I think so. Some poor guy had to choose between two doors. The wrong choice made him a tiger's dinner."

"I have a choice for you."

"What choice?"

"Call it a divorce present . . . or a wedding present."

"Which one is the tiger?"

"You have to decide that."

"Make sense, Gina. I thought you'd be in Las Vegas with Bruce by now."

"No. Read the paper on the table."

He held it to the lantern, frowning deeply while he read the few short lines.

"You had this notarized."

"So you'd know it's real, yes."

"Gina, who wrote this?" Jon eyed her suspiciously.

"I did. A man in the little bank let me use his typewriter to do it."

"Do you know what this means? I can divorce you, and you might not get a cent."

"The paper says I refuse to accept a cent. There's a difference," she retorted.

"You're throwing away the chance to be a rich woman."

"I never wanted money from you. The cash that you gave me is there on the table too."

"What about Bruce? Did you call him?"

"Yes."

"And?"

"I told him our marriage plans had been a mistake."

"Did you tell him we were married?"

"Yes."

"Gina, don't make me drag this out of you one word at a time. What happened with Bruce, and why are you here?"

"Bruce asked me to come to Las Vegas. He said we

185

could have a honeymoon before his cruise and worry about getting married later."

"Even though he knew you were married to me?" he asked bitterly.

"Bruce is broadminded that way." She felt her confidence growing, but her anxious moments weren't over yet.

"That bastard!"

Surprised at his reaction, she wanted to finish talking about Bruce.

"Bruce doesn't believe you married me for revenge. He laughed at the idea."

"Of course, he did," Jon snapped. "I have to look after him because he got the charm and I got the common sense."

"Don't you want to make your choice?"

She stepped out of her sandals, feeling small and helpless as she looked up at his greater height. Carefully she loosened her robe, letting the soft terry cloth slip from her shoulders, but holding it securely over her breasts.

"Don't play games, Gina," he warned hoarsely.

"You asked me if there was any game I was good at."

"Are you sure you can win this one?"

"No, but I'm sure I'll regret it for the rest of my life if I don't try. Your choice, Jon? You can keep my divorce agreement, lock it safely in your metal box, and keep your wealth intact. I'll never make another demand on you."

"Or?"

"Or you can burn it in the stove and claim your wedding gift."

"A hot bath?"

"More than that."

She could hear his sharp intake of breath, but she was too frightened to look at his face. Her whole life depended on what he did in the next few seconds.

What was taking him so long? She was offering him her life, her love, all that a woman could give a man. Would he choose instead a piece of paper that protected his riches?

He moved so close that his shadow became one with hers.

"There can only be the two of us in my bed," he said quietly. "That's one place I won't share with Bruce."

"Not even his shadow will be there, Jon. It never was."

"I want to believe that."

"You can."

He turned his back and moved away while she seesawed between joy and despair.

"Come here," he ordered.

Fumbling awkwardly to slip into her sandals again, she pulled her robe over her shoulders and clutched it under her neck.

"This is the craziest ultimatum I've ever heard," he said severely.

Standing beside the stove as motionless as a marble statue, he held her agreement in front of him as though it had a life of its own. The glare from the stove played over his features as he used a poker to put aside one burner cover. The flames ignited the flimsy paper instantly, making an orange torch that quickly turned to gray curls.

"Done," he said with a strange note in his voice.

Looking at her as if to say it was her turn, he grinned wickedly.

"Does my choice include a back scrubbing?"

"If that's what you want."

"I want it all," he said, bending to press warm lips against hers, but not taking her in his arms.

One thing was missing. Slowly, dully, she turned away and went to the round plastic pool, now more than half filled with mounds of tiny bubbles. Keeping her back turned, she inched her robe off her shoulders, letting it fall where it would until it covered her feet in a crumpled pile. Keeping her face averted, she stepped into the water,

187

stooping to fish for the giant sponge lost from sight in the suds.

With her back toward him, she squeezed the sponge over her shoulders, letting the water cascade down her back and over her breasts, watching tiny drops slide back into the sudsy surface.

"Is it fair to give a gift and use it first?" he asked.

He took the sponge from her, and she sensed, rather than saw, that he'd removed his clothes.

"Or maybe there was a string attached to this gift?" he asked, lowering himself beside her, making the little pool seem crowded as the bubbles rose nearer the rim.

When she didn't answer, he pressed the sponge into her hand and turned his back toward her so her legs couldn't avoid pressing against his hips.

Filling the sponge with warm, sudsy water, she scrubbed the broad expanse of his back, the skin turned honey-tan in the flickering light of the lantern.

"Ah, higher," he moaned. Then again, "Much harder."

She wasn't good at this kind of game; he outfoxed her, outwitted her, outplayed her. Nothing was different from how it had been before she left; his pleasure made her feel empty, at loose ends.

"Did you burn the right paper this time?" she challenged, dropping the sponge and massaging the slippery ridge of his spine.

"Oh, you saw the sketch."

He turned toward her just as she was lifting the water-laden sponge. She pushed it dead center against his face, blinding him with suds and leaving him to sputter while she leaped from the tub.

"I see I chose the tiger," he said as he groped for her discarded robe to rub his smarting eyes, giving her just enough time to wrap a towel around her torso.

He laughed before he lunged out of the pool, capturing

her in an instant, soaking her towel as he wrapped his wet arms around her and pressed her forcefully against him.

"I love you," he said, assaulting her mouth with a powerful, gripping kiss.

"That's all you ever had to say," she grasped, locking her hands behind his neck.

"I couldn't be a substitute for my brother."

"Oh, no, you were never that, Jon. I love you. I have loved you. Only you."

"You may have to spend the next hundred years of your life convincing me."

"No, I can convince you more quickly than that."

She tugged the towel free, but didn't drop it, holding it between them like a matador's cape. When he pulled her into his arms, the length of terrycloth was caught between them, held there by the pressure of their bodies. His hands traveled down her spine, leaving a tingling trail, then cupped her bottom so firmly that she squirmed.

"Convince me," he said in a stranger's voice.

He released her so suddenly that she nearly fell to the floor with the towel, saving herself only because his arm was there to clutch.

"Jon . . ."

"Convince me," he said relentlessly.

For a moment she felt daunted by his aggressive masculinity, intimidating and demanding in a new and terribly exciting way. She put up an arm to shield her breasts from his piercing stare, but the hardness of her nipples against her soft inner arm made the gesture seem childish. She was a woman in love, a married woman, and the man before her was challenging the very essence of her femininity.

She knew she was still afraid to risk giving herself totally to a man, but with the realization she grew stronger, bolder, surer. A shudder passed through her body, but it was a cleansing convulsion, freeing her once and for all of of childhood self. For the first time in her life she reveled in being a woman, a woman able to receive Jon's love.

Taking his hand in both of hers, she led him to the lower bunk where he silently continued his passive role while she peppered him with hard little kisses, loving the hardness of his body and the promise locked in his firm muscles. Exploring, teasing, and touching, they played their game until the intensity of their love became unbearable. She cried out without self-consciousness, and his groans of pleasure mingled with her sharper outbursts until their symphony of love built to a deafening, blinding finale. When at last, flesh and spirits still entwined, they rested, Gina felt a hot tear sliding down her cheek.

"I've made you cry," he said, so distressed he sat up anxiously.

"No, you haven't," she said quickly, sitting and entangling him in a knot of arms and legs. "I'm just so happy I want to boil over."

His lips on hers were tender, warm, loving; his hands lightly stroking her breasts to soothe, not arouse her.

"You've convinced me," he said softly, feigning embarrassment at his confession, burying his face in the damp tendrils of hair at her nape.

"No, I'm sure I haven't. It may take years to do the job properly."

"It may at that," he agreed, "but be sure you'll have your chances."